# The Sun and The Moon

## Possession

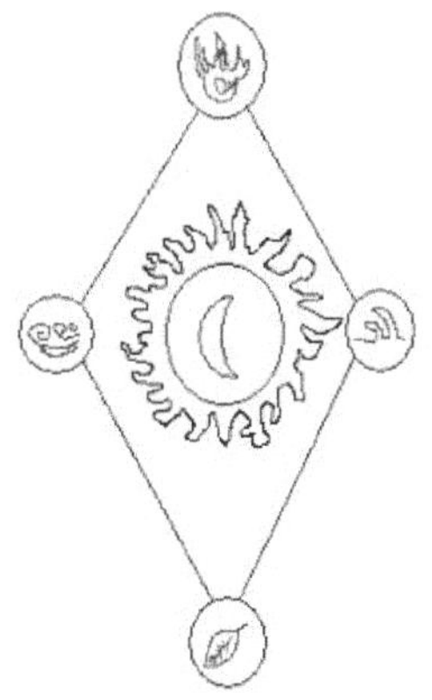

*All characters and events in this publication, other than those clearly in the public domain, are fictitious and any resemblance to real persons, living or dead, is purely Coincidental.*



A CIP catalogue record for this book is available from the British Library.

Published by Creative Publications
www.creative-publications.co.uk

ISBN: 9781912641994

# POSSESSION

# CHAPTER 1

This is a story of how I died. Wow that's a bit strong to start my story but it's true and here's the kicker, I'm not actually dead.
How do I start this, once upon a time, hi, hello, dear diary? I'm going with hello.
Hello my name is Felix and I'm an avatar with a twist but I will get to that later.
How do I describe myself? well, I'm 15, I will be 16 in a few weeks (oh the joy of faking excitement for my parent's benefit).
I'm a little over 6ft tall with short dirty blond hair and grey eyes, well they're more silver than grey, yes you did hear me right I have silver/grey eyes. I would say I'm plain, I'm not big on sports or computers or anything. To be honest, I just like hanging with my two best friends Sean and Karl.
They love all the fantasy and supernatural things like witches, wizards, fairy's, magic, vampires, werewolves you name it they love it as long as it sounds mystical.
Me, on the other hand, I'm not a huge believer but I just go along with it as it gives a meaning to all the weird things happening.
My family, well what can I say about my family apart from their all flipping nuts well apart from my little brother Freddy but he's only 3 so he still has time to get screwed up.

I have twin older brothers known as 'the Satan twins' or Red and Ben that would work too.
They are full-on goth, I don't get it! I get all the black and the death metal music but the make-up and the platform boots? what man would wear it and don't get me started on how they can walk without falling over? On girls, make-up looks really hot but on boys not so much.
My mum Sue is stuck in the 50's, she thinks a woman's place is at the home cooking and cleaning.
My dad also known as Phil is never around, he's always working but when he isn't all he talks about is when he was younger. The story's he tells sound like they come out of a fairy tale, always about bloody fairies and witches. Needless to say, Sean and Karl love him and soak up every last word he says.
When I was younger I thought my dad was a secret agent traveling the world and doing missions as I wouldn't see him for days on end, but I know now his not, he owns a hardware store in the local town.
We live in a cul-de-sac called Arch Close in a little town called Newport Falls that has a population of a little over 2000.
Well, that's me and my family the Moon's.

# CHAPTER 2

My story starts like any other day with my mum shouting up the stairs in her happy cheerful voice!
"Felix time to get up, breakfast is in 10 minutes",
same old routine, get-up, shower, get dressed in jeans and some sort of t-shirt with a band on, today is Green Day.
Then like I always do, I go downstairs and eat far too much breakfast as mum never takes no for an answer.
"You're a growing boy and breakfast is the most important meal of the day, you need to set an example for Freddy".
"Why me? what about the Satan twins?" "they're not at the table and Felix I wish you wouldn't call them that," Mum replied while pilling more bacon on to my plate.
Going back upstairs dodging the Satan twins on the way, I went to the bathroom that is attached to my bedroom to brush my teeth and hair. I say 'brush' what I really mean is I made sure it wasn't sticking up everywhere.
"Have a good day at school" Mum shouted as I was running downstairs to wait outside for Karl and his brother Nick to come and pick me up and take me to the other boring place which people call school.
Today was the same as every other Monday morning at school, I met up with Sean and talked about the recent animal attack "it was a vampire, I'm telling you it's a

conspiracy there trying to cover it up" said Sean.
"Don't be silly Sean, remember what I told you? there's no such thing as vampires or anything supernatural for that matter" I said while shaking my head when something court my eye.
A girl, with long black hair and blonde tips, she looks short about 5.5 and looks really slenderly built.
Next to her was a boy around the same height as me, which was about 6.2 with blond hair he was big built at least twice my size.
I couldn't see their faces just their backs, but something was pulling me to them while fighting against it I was pulled back by a voice.
"Felix are you listing to me?" Karl asked tugging at my arm
"erm no, I wasn't who are they?" I asked while pointing over to them.
"They are the new kids, I'm surprised you don't know them they just moved into your street number 23 I think" "that's the house next to mine. I didn't know the Locks had moved" I said puzzled.
"Get with it, Felix, you really need to wake up and start paying attention," said Karl laughing.
They carried on talking but I just tuned them out staring in the direction the new kids went hopping to see them again, or should I say see her again.

# CHAPTER 3

The morning lessons dragged, science, maths, and then P.E. I hate P.E I know it's meant to be good for you, but I don't really like sports like I said earlier it's not my thing.
At lunch, I met up with Sean and Karl in the cafeteria, they were still going on about the attack in the woods.
While eating my chips thinking about nothing, in particular, something told me to look left, I don't know why but I felt I had no other choice but to look and there they were the new kids walking into the room.
I still couldn't see her face, but I could see his.
He was good looking for a boy, he would totally fit in with the cool kids. Me, Sean and Karl were no way near cool enough, we were more classed as the outcasts. I could see they were having a heated dissuasion as he was pointing at her and shaking his head.
All I could think about was going over there to protect her, I could feel the anger bubbling up inside of me towards the new boy.
I hadn't noticed that I had stood up "where you are going Felix?" asked Sean, I shook my head "nowhere" "well sit down then" he replied. While slowly sitting I couldn't take my eyes off them, the girl looked different, but I couldn't put my finger on it.

"Stop staring Felix, you want to get a beating or something," asked Karl trying to catch my eye by waving his hands in front of my face "I've got to go," I said standing up and nearly running out the cafeteria. Karl and Sean were shouting after me, but I just had to get out of there.

Sitting at the back of the football field I could barely hear the bell go off to let me know lunch has ended 'Great double art' I thought to myself, it's one of the only subjects I like in school, art, music, and history. I know I know history is a bit of a geeky subject, but I like it, so get over it.

While walking into the art room I focused on my table as I have it all to myself well, so I thought.

I could see the new girl at my table, she is the most beautiful girl I've ever seen. Her skin was flawless it looked so soft, I really wanted to touch it but I hadn't even spoken to her.

So, I think touching her would be crossing the line and with her brother 'no thank you!'.

I couldn't see her eyes as they were looking down at the table, as I pulled my chair back it screeched across the floor (dam nothing like bringing attention to myself) "Mr. Moon please hurry and sit down we've got a lot to get through today".

"Yes sir" I replied, Mr. Gary was my maths teacher, he was just covering as Mrs. Homes was away and (I get the vibe) he really didn't like me very much.

Once I sat I got my book and pencil out of my bag and started doodling a picture of a symbol.

I couldn't tell you how I know it but it's the only thing I draw. It's like a diamond shape with a fire at the top, waves to the right, wind to the left and at the bottom is a leaf but in the middle of the diamond is a sun with a half crescent moon inside it.

"Wow that's nice" a low voice whispered, I looked up to see a pair of golden eyes looking back at me.
I couldn't speak I felt frozen all I could do was stare at her.
She smiled back at me, and all I could feel was butterflies in my stomach, I felt drawn to her.
Shaking my head trying to compose myself "erm it's just a drawing, I can't help myself from drawing it sometimes, why am I telling you this? Hi, I'm Felix Moon."
Her eyes widened and a panic and scared looked crossed her face "hi" she said quickly and just looked back down at the desk letting her hair fall over her face.
'Ok, let's pretend that wasn't weird' I thought.
Throughout the lesson I sneaked a few looks her way, I couldn't stop myself. She looked different then it hit me the tips of her hair was light brown not blonde like they were this morning.
She was still looking down, I don't think she has looked up all lesson while watching her texting on her phone I noticed Mr. Gary coming our way.
I couldn't help myself from coughing and whispering, "Mr. Gary's coming, put it away or you're going to lose it".
She quickly slid it in her jeans pocket, "What are you doing

here Felix? this doesn't look like the task I just set you."
Mr. Gary said while picking my sketchbook up and ripping the page out that I had just drawn, he screwed it up and dropped it back on my desk and walked off.
Just as he approached his desk the bell rang to let us know that the lesson has finished.
I put my stuff back in my bag and left the screwed-up picture on the table.
As I walked towards the door normally being the last one out, I glanced back at the table to see the new girl putting my picture in her bag 'that's strange' I thought.
Karl and Sean approached catching me staring, I only looked away just for a second to say 'hi' but when I looked back she was gone.
'Where did she go?' I thought, I was standing in the only doorway to the classroom.

# CHAPTER 4

On the car journey home, I couldn't stop thinking about her, it was like a switch that I couldn't turn off.
Once I arrived home I just stood in the front garden staring at the house next door, I couldn't tear myself away. All of a sudden, the new girl appeared in one of the top windows 'how on earth did she get home before me' I thought as I quickly looked away.
I walked up the garden path and pushed the front door open "Mum I'm home" I shouted, "I'm in the kitchen my love" she replied, where else would she be?
I could smell she was baking "what you are cooking?" "an apple pie" after walking into the kitchen I picked up Freddy "hi fella did you have a good day at school?" he told me about his day, painting, playing outside with his friends and story time, Freddy loves story time.
"Hey, Mum did you know the Locks from next-door moved out?" "yes, that's why I've baked this pie, its a welcome gift to the street" Mum replied.
Freddy tapped me on the shoulder "me hun-gy" Freddy said "come on mini-me let's get you some food" I said walking over to the fridge. I made Freddy a ham sandwich and grabbed myself a drink.
While walking up the stairs my Mum shouted, "we are going

next door at 5 so don't go to sleep!" "ok, Mum whatever" I replied.
Whilst laying on my bed I felt this strange pull towards the need to go next door. I have never felt this feeling before, like ever! before today anyway, I still don't even know her name.
A part of me didn't want to go, I keep thinking about the scared look on her face when she heard my name. "FELIX ITS TIME" my Mum shouted up the stairs, I got up off my bed and went down the stairs "why do I have to go as well? the Satan twins sorry, Red and Ben Ent here nor is Dad."
"Because the twins are out, and your father is at work".
We walked down our small garden path and up theirs, Freddy seemed to become more scared the closer we got to the house, "it's ok Freddy" I said picking him up and putting him on my back, so he could hide if he wants to.
He's always been really shy with new people, his fingers were twisting and twirling in my hair, it's something he has always done but recently when he twiddles it, it feels different, it feels like my whole body is slightly humming, I have learned to just ignore it.
My Mum rang the doorbell and a huge man answered, he was cleanly shaven apart from a small goatee with deep blue eyes, he must be 6ft 9 at least and he was big built.
His mussels seemed to be everywhere 'note to self, DO NOT piss this dude off'.
Freddy quickly hid behind me "hello, I'm Sue Moon and these are two of my boys, Felix and Freddy. I've brought you this pie to say welcome to the neighborhood" but when my mum said my name the huge bloke looked at me like he wanted to kill me.
'What the hell have I done? I've never seen this dude before!'.

"Well thank you, Mrs. Moon, please come in, I'm Calvin Redfield, KIDS" Calvin shouted up the stairs. There she was appearing in the doorway, the beautiful girl from school. The tips of her hair were black like the rest of her hair, how weird 'she must colour it in with those hair pens as no one's hair changes colour that fast from blond to brown to black' I was confused.

"This is my son Chadwick, and this is my daughter Star, Kids these are the Moons, Sue, Freddy and Felix" Chadwick's eyes nearly popped out his head.

'What is it with these people with my name, as soon as they hear it they all look freaked out', "nice to meet you, Mrs. Moon, Dad I've got a load of homework" said Chadwick his Dad just nodded.

"Shall we? this pie smells delicious" said Calvin leading us to the living room. Me and Freddy sat on the single chair together as Freddy wouldn't get off my back, so I just left him there.

My Mum sat on the same sofa as Calvin, "So you said they were just two of your sons?" Calvin questioned.

"Oh yes I have twin boys Red and Ben they are 17, My husband Phil owns the little hardware store in town.

So, is there a Mrs. Redfield?" Mum asked.

"No Anna passed away a few years ago," he said softly.

"Oh, I'm so sorry to hear that," my Mum said putting her hand on his shoulder, "it's ok it was a while ago now, but thank you" Calvin replied.

All of a sudden there was a loud bang that followed a crash, Freddy screamed and started crying gripping hold of my shoulders.

"Star go and see if Chadwick is ok," Calvin asked. "Ok Dad" she sounded bitter as though she was annoyed that she had to leave.

"Mum I'm going to take Freddy home," I said while standing up "no he will be ok just sit back down," said Mum in a sharp tone.

My Mum shocked me, she never speaks to me like that, saying that she never touches anyone she doesn't know.

I slowly sat back down while Freddy was still crying hiding behind me.

After a few minutes, Star walked back into the room "Chadwick's fine just tripped over some clothes".

'Well that was a crap lie' I don't know how I knew but I knew she was lying, just like when Chadwick said he's got homework to do. I knew that was a lie too, all these new feelings started after meeting her.

My Mum and Calvin talked for what felt like hours, I stayed silent as did Star still standing behind her dad, "Well its getting late my husband will be getting home soon and needs feeding as do the boys, if you need anything don't hesitate to come over" mum said while walking towards the door. "Thank you, Mrs. Moon," said Calvin opening the front door, "please call me Sue" mum replied, "ok thank you, Sue".

Mum and I began to walk down the pathway, just before turning towards our house I turned back, Calvin was looking at me with an evil look in his eye.

I couldn't move my head back quick enough, I couldn't stop myself looking back for the second time and there she was Star in one of the upstairs windows, she was smiling down at me.

I gave her a little wave just before she closed the blind.

After dinner, I took Freddy to my room for a bit because Freddy likes the colours that my room light up in, yellows, red, golds from the setting sun it's like fire dancing around my room.

Freddy had fallen asleep on my bed, so I couldn't sit down

as I didn't want to wake him so I walked over to my window and sat on the ledge, I swing my legs over the ledge do I was facing out side and they were dangling outside.
My Mum hates it when I do it, but I like the feeling of the sun setting on my face and my feet dangling free, kind of feels like flying.
While looking down into next-doors garden I could see Star standing there, arms spread out, eyes closed, head tilted all the way back and she was saying something in a low voice.
I couldn't hear what she was saying so I just sat there looking at her, staring more like, I just couldn't take my eyes off her.
"What you are doing you little freak?" a voice said behind me "nothing" I snapped back.
"Who's that?" Ben said poking his head out the window "she's no one" "she doesn't look like no one, not the way you're gorping at her. HAY YOU, MY BROTHER LOVES YOU." shouted Ben pulling his head back in the window, so he couldn't be seen.
Star looked up with a furious expression on her face, I quickly got back in the window and stood "there was no need for that Ben" I said pushing him out of my room and slamming the door.
I walked back to the window and peeked my head out, but she was gone.
So, I shut my window and got on with my maths homework.
A little while later I heard a soft voice, "Felix is Freddy in there with you?" Mum said while gently knocking on my door.
I got up from my computer chair and opened the door "he's asleep on my bed Mum" I replied while letting her in to get him.
"Mum I think that the new neighbors are really weird," I said in a questing tone "oh god Felix they have only just moved in

I think they're really nice so don't cause any trouble. I mean it Felix just leave them alone".

Mum said while picking Freddy up and walking out of my room.

By the time I finished my homework, it was only 9:23 pm, so I put my headphones in and listened to Hurricane by 30 Seconds to Mars.

Opening my window and dangling my feet out like earlier, completely forgetting about the incident with my stupid brother's earlier, I was listening to music while looking out up towards the stars daydreaming when my phone went off, it made me jump so much I slipped off the ledge and started to fall towards the ground.

It happened so fast I couldn't turn and grab the ledge in time before I could shout for help all of a sudden, I had stopped falling. I could feel my feet land on something hard but looking down there was nothing but air.

I quickly stretched up to reach the window frame to help me pull myself up and climb back in, I was so scared I could feel my hands and arms shaking.

After pulling myself up and through my window I fell on the bedroom floor while lying there I couldn't help thinking that I could have killed myself, broken both of my legs or back and never be able to walk again!

I crawled back to the window and poked my head back out, was I going crazy? I was trying to find where I had landed and still, nothing was there, my eyes started to wander around looking to see if anyone saw what had happened.

In the new neighbor's garden was Star staring straight at me with her eyes wide open like she just saw a ghost and her jaw nearly touching the floor.

"Hey! did you just see that?" I shouted, she just shook her head letting her hair fall over her face and quickly walked

back towards her house, ‘ok now that girl is officially weird’ I thought while closing my window.
It was Sean that had texted me that nearly ended my boring life.

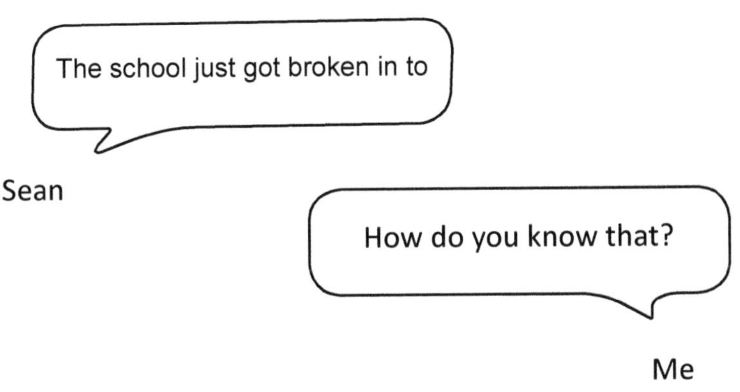


After I pressed send the message I felt stupid as I know full well that Sean’s Dad is the sheriff, he knows everything that goes on in this small town.

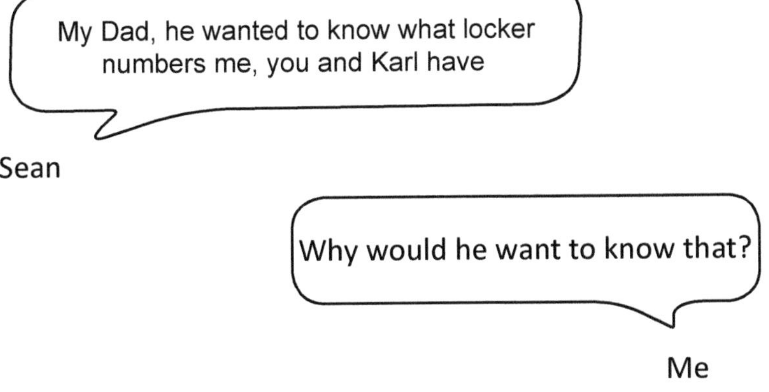

I don't know maybe that's what got broken into. He just said there was a break in at the school.

Sean

Well we will have to see at school tomorrow

Me

I was debating on telling him what just happened but I didn't really know myself so I thought against it as it would have sounded stupid and crazy.

It took me ages to fall asleep the adrenalin was still pumping threw me and gave me a cracking headache, so I took two Co-codamol knowing full well that they will knock me straight out.

# CHAPTER 5

In the morning I followed the same routine, get up, shower, get dressed, breakfast, brush hair and teeth then go wait for Karl and his brother to come and pick me up for school in the front garden.

The only different thing this morning was my window, it was wide open when I woke I could have sworn I shut it last night after the incident, but I just brushed it off.

When I got out of the car at school everyone was looking at me "why is everyone looking at me like that?" I asked, "because you're weird," replied Karl's brother Nick slamming his car door and walking off.

Sean came running up to us and said, "oh my god I can't believe it can you?" in a questionable tone. "Sean, slow down mate I don't know what you are talking about," I said while walking towards him. "Felix your locker got broken into, just yours no one else's".

I didn't believe it, so I bolted to where my locker is whilst approaching it I could see all the people crowded around. Principal York and sheriff Hardy were standing there talking, my locker door was ripped clean off all twisted and mangled laying on the floor and my books were all over the place.

"Felix can you come to my office please, everyone else you can go to class now," said Principal York.

I walked to his office in a daze 'why would someone do something like that? my locker was ripped apart no way of fixing it' I couldn't help thinking to myself while walking behind the Principal and the Sheriff, everyone was still staring at me.
In the office they were asking me the same questions over and over again, who do you think done it? have I annoyed anyone? What was in my locker? I hadn't got a clue who or even why someone would do it and I only had my school books in my locker nothing valuable.
I probably could have scraped £2 together with what was in my locker, they let me go to class after an hour of their stupid questions.
At lunch I sat down with Sean and Karl (like always)
"I've got something to tell you two, I can't keep it to myself anymore, but you can't make a big deal out of it" I said in a hushed tone, they just nodded giving me the go head to continue.
"Last night when you texted me, Sean, I was sitting on the window ledge daydreaming with my headphones in and the text rang so loud it made me jump, literally made me jump and I fell off the ledge."
I could see the shock in the faces "oh crap, are you ok? sorry mate" said Sean.
"I'm here Ent I, I'm fine I didn't fall far my feet landed on something, but it was some sort of invisible ledge" they both looked shocked and questionable at the same time. They didn't speak for a few minutes, they both just sat in silence, then all of sudden Karl broke it "so you're telling us that you fell out your second story window and landed on an invisible ledge? could your clothes just of got caught on something?" I shook my head "no I had no shoes on and I could feel it under my feet, the new girl witnessed it, I need

to find her and talk to her, but I can't see her anywhere" I said while scanning the cafeteria trying to locate her perfect face but still no luck.
I couldn't even see her brother Chadwick and he's not hard to miss,
Sean and Karl were still looking stumped. Something supernatural happened last night and they don't know what to do with the information I just told them.
The rest of the day there was still no sign of the new kids, I even made sure I was the first person outside so I could catch her leaving but I didn't see either of them.
Once I got home I went straight next-door and knocked, I don't know what I'm going to say when I see her but I need to see her to talk.
Mr. Redfield opened the door "hello Mr. Redfield, is Star home?" I asked in a cheerful tone, "no she's not back from school yet" he said in a really angry tone and shut the door in my face, causing a loud bang.
I previously had a strong feeling that he was lying about something but this time I really did know, why he would lie? Star and Chadwick were both missing from school today.
While walking down their pathway making my way home, I notice the Satan twins arrive home "woo what you doing over there freak?" shouted Red.
"That's rich coming from you two, weird and weirder" I shouted back, "so was your girlfriend there?" Red asked making kissy noises with his lips "or did she dump you because you're a huge looser" said Ben. "She Ent my girlfriend, anyway I don't see you two with girlfriends so stay out of my love life," I said storming up the stairs and slamming my door.
'That's strange! I thought I shut that this morning?' I thought while now looking at the window that's wide open again.

Looking around my room I could see it was messier than normal, also I could smell lavender, it was so strong my nose tingled.

I couldn't understand as the window was wide open, I assumed the smell came from the field just out of town as lavender grew there.

As it seemed a little breezy I presumed the wind had blown the strong fragrance in my room, it happened from time to time. "Someone's been in my room," I said out loud. I looked around, but nothing was missing, then I remembered Freddy was home from pre-school today, so it could have been him.

So that was all the that happened that week saying that even the week after was about the same as before I met Star, uneventful.

I still looked for Star during school, every day was the same outcome.

I never once saw her, not even during our lesson together on a Monday.

# CHAPTER 6

So, it was the week of my birthday and my Mum asked me at least once a day "what do you want for your sweet 16th birthday?" there's nothing I really wanted other than a new phone, I already know my parents are throwing me a surprise party, Karl had already let slip that it's a pool party and everyone is invited.

Even people I don't like, the Redfield's had an invite even though I still haven't seen Star or Chadwick at school. I'm not even sure they will even bother coming after their father slammed the door in my face!

It was Thursday (the day before my special birthday) still no sign of Star it's like she has just up and disappeared or never existed in the first place.

Everyone had forgotten the locker fiasco and moved on with their boring lives, the head had moved me to a locker near Karl, so when I walked towards my new locker I noticed I had five birthday cards stuck to the front.

Even though I'm not a cool kid I still get cards from random people it makes me a little happy inside to know that people bothered to write me a card, who even does that nowadays? I pulled them off and opened my locker door, I exchanged the cards for my history books, I closed my locker making sure that it was shut properly. While doing so Chadwick

caught my eye, I quickly walked over to him trying not to seem like a weirdo stalker.
“Hey Chadwick, could I have a minute please?” I said a bit afraid no petrified, that’s the word I’m looking for and I really didn’t know what to say to him.
He just waved his hand and the people he was with just walked away “what?” Chadwick asked aggressively ‘oh god he’s going to kill me’ ‘run, run you fool’ my brain was telling me, but I wanted to know where Star was “err I was just wondering where is Star? It’s just she hasn’t been to school for a while and every time I come over your Dad says she’s at school” I asked in a nervous tone.
“It’s none of your business and if I was you I would just drop it, Star can get very touchy when people get in her way” he said while stepping closer, you know that close you could feel his breath on your face “So, stop” he whispered in my ear with a strong demanding tone.
He was so close to my face I could feel the heat off him on my face.
All of a sudden, the doors burst open and what felt like a hurricane blew through the halls. It blew everyone around me over but not me, it was like the wind was protecting me from Chadwick, after pushing everyone away from me.
The wind disappeared as fast as it had come, all of a sudden, I heard Lea Faith scream I looked over in her direction, she was laying on the floor holding her head.
There were books and paper all over the floor, people were getting back to their feet with shocked looks on their faces.
I looked back at Chadwick, he was still on the floor looking at me with more anger in his face that I’ve ever seen on anyone. I couldn’t help but run, I ran as fast as I could to my next lesson, history.
In history I couldn’t stop thinking about what happened in

the corridor, 'it has to of been something I did as it never touched me?', I looked at my hands shaking my head.
Don't ask me why I did what I did next as I couldn't tell you why, but I blew into my left hand, all of a sudden, my breath became a ball of wind in my hand, twisting and turning.
I could feel my heart pounding in my chest as I was staring at it, it scared the living hell out of me.
I slammed my hands on the table and pushed my chair back, the leg caught the table leg tipping me backwards. "Mr. Moon try and stay awake in my class please," said Mr. Park in an annoyed tone, everyone just looked and laughed at me getting off the floor.
"Sorry sir," I said as a picked up my chair and sat back at my table, I couldn't stop my hands from shaking. Once everyone turned back to look towards the front of the class I couldn't help trying it again.
At the beginning of lunch, I walked towards Sean and Karl who were sitting in our usual spot.
They were talking about the 'hall hurricane', this is what all of the students are calling it "I think I'm going mad" I said as I sat down with a bump.
"Why? what's up mate?" asked Sean while giving me my lunch as he knows I have history at the other side of the school and the lunch queue is always busy.
One time I had to queue for 30 minutes while some girls were discussing whether to have a salad or a skinny latte for lunch! "I don't know how to describe it, but I think I caused the wind in the halls," I said shaking my head in disbelief.
Sean and Karl just laughed I mean really gut-wrenching, belly moving laughed, "what on earth are you going on about? It was a freak accident" said Sean with a huge smile on his face.
"I've got to show you something but not here." Let's go to the field" I said grabbing my food and walking out of the

cafeteria, Sean and Karl looked confused but followed me.

# CHAPTER 7

We walked to the very far end of the field where no one could see us "come on Felix what you got to show that's so important that you have taken us this far away from school?" asked Karl in an annoyed tone, "I don't want anyone to see it.
You know I keep telling you two that magical things don't exist well cheek this out." I said putting my hand out "Felix we don't have time for this we are going to be late" Karl said as he began to walk away "Karl just trust me and wait" Karl stopped and turned towards me, I blew gently in my hand and it happened again my breath became a ball of wind twisting and turning in my hand.
Sean and Karl were shocked both of their mouths dropped that far open they may as well be on the floor. Sean put his hand out to touch the wind orb that's still spinning in my hand "can I touch it?" he said in a questionable tone.
"Go ahead I don't know what it will do though" Sean reached out and gently touched it, suddenly it split in half one of the sides shot straight out of my hand and hit Sean in the chest, he went flying a good 10ft away from where we were standing. I clapped my hands together to extinguish the last of the wind orb.
"Sean I'm so sorry I didn't know that was going to happen," I

said pancaking that I had hurt him, "it's ok mate it hurt don't get me wrong but that was the coolest thing ever!" he said. So, for the rest of the day, we didn't go to any classes we just stayed in the field playing with the wind.

We were trying all sorts of things to control the wind orb, speaking to it, waving their hands through it. By the end of school, I could pick Sean up a foot high off the floor with one hand while pushing Karl away with the wind ball I created in my other. But once one of them laughed I lost my concentration, the wind ball would disappear from my hand, "Felix this is so cool" said Sean standing back up as I had dropped him when I lost my concentration.

"I know but why is this happening, it's so weird," I said clapping my hands together. "Maybe you can talk to someone?" said Sean, "like who Sean? like who? You two are the only people that know and that's how I want to keep it, don't mind being a freak between us three but if it got out my life would be hell. Honestly, who would believe me anyway?" "we won't tell anyone will we?" Sean said while looking at Karl, he just shook his head.

"Come on or we will miss our ride home," Karl said as he began to walk towards the school.

At home, I followed my normal boring routine just, so it looked like another normal day.

While in my room I began playing with the wind orb in my hands letting it bounce from one hand to the other, all of a sudden, my door flung open, I quickly clapped my hands together, so no one could see what I was doing.

It was Sean and Karl with loads of books in their hands, "we think we know what you are" said Karl all exited "shhh someone might hear" I said while jumping up and shutting the door "well me and Sean have been looking in all of these books and have come to the conclusion that you

have aerokinesis" he said in a much to exited tone "what's that then?" I asked.
"It's exactly what you are doing, controlling the wind with your mind, this is so cool. How long do you think you have had it? because the book says people are born with it" said Karl.
"I don't know, I've only just discovered it," I said while looking at my hands "what about that thing a few weeks ago where you fell out the window? you said you were saved by air!" said Sean while peering out the window looking down towards the ground.
He was right that did happen "you know what, do you two remember when we were 9 and we would play in the Drake Forest and I was up that tree and fell, I hit my head on that rock? well, there was a huge gust of wind that day as well just like the one at school today" I said deep in thought.
"How could we forget, you died, you stopped breathing and had no pulse for like five minutes.
That was the scarcest day of my life!" said Sean shaking his head in disbelief. "Well ever since then just little things have happened like windows flying open when I'm angry, but I never thought anything of it," I said while trying to think of other instances.
The rest of the night they were telling me that I didn't need to blow in my hand to get the wind orb I can draw it from the sky. It was really hard in the house, I tried to pull it in through the window, but it looked really strange, I'm sure people would notice a tunnel of wind coming out of my window, so I just stuck with blowing in my hand for now.
Sean and Karl went home around 7 pm, as I felt drained I tries to sleep all I could think of is 'how have I got this power and none in the family have' I couldn't understand, 'I'm not special in any way' "Dad" I said while jumping off my bed

and running down stairs.
"Where do you think you are going, mister?" said my Mum with Freddy in her arms on her way to put Freddy to bed
"I need to talk to Dad" I said while grabbing my trainer and sliding my right foot in.
"Can't you wait till he comes home?" she said over her shoulder, "no, it's a man thing" I said after putting my left trainer on and bolting to the door, she did say something after but I ran so fast I never heard it.
I ran all the way to town which wasn't really that far only a 15 minutes run when in full sprint, I got to the store at just after 8. Inside there was no one in sight.
"Dad are you there?" I shouted, "Felix is that you? what are you doing here?" Dad asked while walking through the door behind the front desk.
"Hey, Dad I need to ask you something and I....." I couldn't finish my sentence, "what's up son?" he asked, I just stood there unable to speak "well if you can't tell me I can't help you" he asked in a worried tone staring down at me, I looked down at my hands and thought 'do I tell him or just show him' "Dad you know the story's you told me when I was younger about fairy's and witches?" I could see in his face that they were true, but I need him to tell me.
"I wanted to know how true they are?" I asked looking him in the eyes, "come and sit down he said while putting a hand on my back guiding me to sit on the counter in front of where I was standing.
"Where's this come from son, you have never really been that interested in my story's?" he said.
While sitting I said, "it's just I remember you telling me this one story about a fairy that can control the water", "Annadora? Felix why are you asking me about her?" he asked in a questionable tone "Dad is it true?" I shouted,

“sorry Dad,” I said jumping off the counter and rubbing my hands over my face shaking my head.
“Err well my Granddad your Great Granddad said he knew her and she was pure evil, nothing good came from her but I think it’s all just stories,” my Dad said with a confused and worried expression on his face.
“So, are all the fairy’s evil or is it just the one that possessed the water power?” I asked, “he told me that not all the fairies are good most of them are, Annadora is another category of evil she just kills for the sake of killing it’s like a sport for her. Felix, please tell me why you want to know about her?” but as I was just about to answer him Mr. Cole from the sweet shop next-door come in the shop.
“Are you ready Phil, oh sorry I didn’t know you had company?” he said.
“It’s ok Mr. Cole, Dad I will see you at home” I reached for the door handle and pulled the door open, I couldn’t help but leg it as quick as I could. “Felix, FELIX” my Dad called after me, but I was gone.
At home I just went straight to my room, as soon as I shut the door there was a knock “Felix” it was my Mum “what Mum?” I asked, “I just want to know if you were hungry?” she asked through the closed door, “no Mum I’m fine I am just tired,” I said while sitting on my bed and taking off my trainers.
“Ok sweetie big day tomorrow get some sleep, night” Mum replied, “night Mum” ‘oh no my birthday I forgot about that’ I tried to sleep but all I did was toss and turn all night.
In the morning I felt like a zombie from living dead, I could barely keep my eyes open while I sat at the breakfast table opening my cards and presents “your new phone is all set up with your old number, all you have to do is put your contacts in” said my Dad while passing me the phone, he was opening

the shop late so he can spend my birthday morning with me. "Thanks, Dad, I love it, I better go and get ready for school". Once upstairs I got dressed and started pacing, I looked out the window and there was Star pacing to in her back garden. I was just about to open the window when my Mum shouted up the stairs that Karl's brother is waiting so I picked up my bag and quickly ran down the stairs and out the door.

While getting in the car and shutting the door Karl looked over his shoulder at me from the front seat "Hey Felix, Happy Birthday" he said in a cheerful tone. "Cheers mate I just can't wait till this day is over" I said while staring out of the window. "But why? I love birthdays" he said "Ok, I will get everyone to say happy birthday to you, deal" Karl just nodded.

School went so fast most of it was a blur, given birthday cards and "see you later at the party" comments became too much.

My last lesson was double art and I've come to the conclusion that Star won't be back at this school 'maybe she's transferred to St Bart's in the next town for really brainy kids', I thought while walking into class and there she was sitting at my desk.

She looked different from the last time I saw her, this time she was looking up, so I can see her beautiful golden eyes like liquid gold, today the tips of her hair were black like the last time I saw her in her garden.

As soon as she spotted me come in the class she smiled directly at me, then quickly looked away out the window.

I sat down and tried to just look ahead but I couldn't, the pull between us was impossible, I couldn't stop looking at her I mean staring at her even I thought I was being weird.

"Mr. Gary has gone home with a sickness bug so with this in mind please can you just get on with homework, my office is

a few doors down, so I can hear you all, I will keep popping in to check on you," said Principal York then he left the room. I just folded my arms across the table and laid my head on them, I was so tired but I couldn't sleep knowing she was next to me so I purposely faced away from her, I could feel her eyes burning in the back of my head, so I turned towards her but keeping my eyes closed.
"Happy Birthday" her beautiful voice whispered, my eyes flu open "are you talking to me?" I asked in a much too excited voice "unless there's someone else who has a birthday today?" Star said with a beautiful smile on her face, I sat up losing my train of thought in her eyes.
I shook my head to clear my mind "no it's just me, thank you" I said. "Here I got this for you," she said while handing me a card with a cake and happy birthday written on the front and inside it read;

*To Felix,*

*Happy*
*16th Birthday*
*sorry I haven't*
*been around*
*I will explain later*
*at the*
*party*

*From Star*

"I don't understand, why won't you tell me now?" I asked in a soft tone, "I could but let's just say I don't have enough power to" Star said putting her hand on the tips of her hair and the subject was dropped.

So, for the rest of the lesson, we spoke about other things like favourite films, favourite music, favourite colour until the subject of the 'hall hurricane' and the 'locker incident' came up.
"So, I've missed a lot since I've been gone?" she asked, "Star I need to ask you something?" Star just nodded to say go ahead, "well do you remember the first day here and when you found out what my name was you looked so freaked out, why was that?" I asked hoping she wouldn't feel uncomfortable and leave.
Star just pointed at the card and said "later, Principal York is coming look busy" she said and then looked down and started to write in her book, so I did the same and just as I put pen to paper there he was at the door 'how the hell did she know that' I looked at my card knowing she will tell me later.
All of a sudden, the bell rang it made both of us jump 'no, no, no, no' I thought I don't want to stop talking, the only time I didn't ever want to leave school was today! "See you later at my party" I said while grabbing my books and placed them in my rucksack, "until then" she said while standing up, she put her hand on my shoulder and the tips of her hair started to change colour ever so slightly, I could see a brown tint mixed in with the black. Star turned and looked at me, puzzled, touching her hair then quickly leaving the classroom.

# CHAPTER 8

All the way home I felt like I was in a daze, Karl and Sean tried to pull me out of it but failed miserably. They were both staying at my house tonight as it's my birthday "you girls have a fantastic slumber party" shouted Nick's brother out the window just before driving off.
"Felix, what is the matter with you? you seem out of it" Sean asked in a questionable tone.
"Ok before we go inside I will tell you, in art I sat next to Star and we spoke about a few things, while talking she gave me this" I pulled the card out of my pocket and unfolded it and showed it to them.
After they both read it Karl said, "what does she mean about telling you later?" "well, she did say that she couldn't explain then as she didn't have enough power to, also when she touched me her hair started to change colour".
It felt as though Sean and Karl couldn't believe what they were hearing as they both just stared at me with a stupid look on their faces. "This is so cool," Karl said giving me back the card.
While walking into my house my parents shouted "surprise" there were banners and balloons everywhere saying 'sweet $16^{th}$ Felix'.
"Wow this is so unexpected I did wonder why Karl and Sean

come home with me," I said in a cheery tone. Wow, my acting skills have gone up a notch Oscars here I come. All three of us went upstairs and got ready for the party.
The party was so boring, but my Mum was loving it so that's all that mattered to me, I love watching her smile. I think everyone from school turned up, I scanned the garden and could see the cheerleaders Sinead, Mercedes and Lexi, a couple of boys from the football team Mason, Brayden, Levi, and Ashton. Even the cool kids Skye, Elliott, Hudson, and Fynn were here, even though I don't talk to half of them I was taken aback that they all bothered to come.
The Satan twins brought some of their Goth friends and even the Redfield's turned up, Calvin went over to talk to my Dad. Chadwick went over to the cool kids and the jocks and Star walked straight to me "happy birthday" she said putting her hand on my shoulder and kissing my cheek, just as her lips touched my face I felt a weird sensation running down my body.
She had her hood up so I couldn't see her hair, but I knew she felt something too as her hand moved off my shoulder rather quickly "err thanks" I said looking into her eyes. She stayed with us for the rest of the party, it ended at 10:30 pm and everyone left, Sean, Karl, and Star were the only ones still here who helped to clean up.
Sean was upstairs cleaning, Karl was in the living room and Star was doing the dishes in the kitchen while I was in the garden.
My Mum would normally do all this kind of stuff took Freddy to bed and had not been back down since, I assumed Freddy hadn't settled, so we all just started to tidy up.
My Dad went over to Calvin's to fix something he did say what but to be honest I really wasn't listening. I was picking up cups when I noticed a man standing at the back of the

garden with a red hooded cloak on that was covering his face, so I couldn't make out if I knew him or not.
I could just about see he had a mark on his hand, it was a gold lightning bolt. "Can I help you mate?" I shouted out in his direction, I started to hesitantly move closer to him.
I knew there was something different about him I could feel it, it's not like the pull I have with Star but it's like the feeling of anger, so much so that I need to hurt him or even kill him I had so much hatred in me.
I was just about to put my hands to my mouth as its the fastest way to get the wind in my hands, but suddenly, I could see him charging towards me.
I didn't have time to react he was so fast, in no time at all he had me pinned up against the fence by my throat, the pressure around my neck felt so painful and I could barely breathe, then I could smell it.
The same lavender smell that I could smell in my room a few weeks ago, I tried to pull his hand away, but it just got tighter. I was now lifted a good foot off the ground, I started to kick out but with his other hand, he had them pinned to the fence.
I couldn't feel him touching them though it must have been magic. 'Magic of bloody course' I thought, I was so mad with myself for not being stronger "why are you doing this?" I struggled to say while still trying to pull his finger's away from my neck.
"I want this," he said, his voice was so dark and full of hatred, then I felt the pressure off my legs, suddenly he made a claw with his hand over my heart and stared chanting in a language I've never heard before in my life! but the pain it gave off oh my god, it hurt so much. Ok think of it this way, think about the worse pain you have ever felt in your whole life then times it by five then times that number

by ten that's about how much pain I'm feeling right now. I tried to shout out but the hold around my throat was so tight I could hardly breathe, I could feel myself starting to lose consciousness when I heard someone shout "Kayos no".

Unexpectedly he released my neck and I was thrown over his shoulder like I was a little girls rag doll. When I landed on the floor I could hear an almighty crack when my head connected with the concrete near the swimming pool, my head felt as though it was going to explode.

Once I pulled myself up and was able to stand I could see it was Star who pulled him away and was now fighting with him. The one she called Kayos, they were speaking in that strange language again, I couldn't make out what they were saying to each other, all of a sudden garden chairs were hurtling towards Kayos.

I tried to walk towards Star to help but the floor was spinning and the next thing I knew I was stumblingly backwards, I couldn't reach out to stop myself. I fell into the pool backward with a big splash! I tried to kick my feet, but I was so confused and dizzy I could barely keep a hold of the side of the pool "help" I tried to shout but every time I did all I got was a mouthful of water.

The water was freezing, it was so cold I couldn't hold on much longer, I could feel myself sinking. I no longer had enough energy to keep my head above the water, my body felt heavy and I could feel myself sinking.

The last thing I remember seeing was the bubbles of my last breath floating out of my mouth and up to the surface, while watching them I couldn't help thinking 'I wish it was that easy to float' I closed my eyes and allowed my body to sink to the bottom of the pool, I was gone.

# CHAPTER 9

I could feel my eyes flicker open, wherever I was I had a strong feeling of Deja vu really bad, "hello" I said out loud feeling really stupid about it as there was nothing around me.

I was in a white room, there wasn't even any windows, doors, nothing. I sat in the corner for what felt like hours, when there was a beautiful bright light in the opposite corner to where I was sitting, it was getting brighter and brighter. It eventually got so bright I had to close my eyes and cover them with my hands, I peeked through my fingers and tried not to look directly into it as my eyes were not stinging.

I was startled when the light suddenly vanished, and all I could see was an old man standing where the light had come from.

He was wearing a light grey toga that looked like it was made from linen, on his feet he wore brown saddles. Honestly, he looked like he was a Greek god "what the, how did you get in here? where am I? how did I get here? how do I get out?" I was starting to freak out I could feel my breathing change, it was much quicker like I was struggling to take in any air. The man just stood there all calm, with his hands by his sides just staring at me freaking out "finished?" he asked. I stood up shakily and began to pace back and forth while trying to breathe deep to calm myself "yes" I said in a whisper, I felt

like that took everything out of me to squeeze that out while trying to calm myself.
"Well Felix haven't you grown since the last time we spoke," he said as a matter of fact! by now I was slightly calmer and had my breathing under control "sorry mate but I don't know you" I said staring at him.
"It was a while ago about 7 years I would say" I just shook my head "I'm Aires, we spoke after you fell from a tree" I froze in my tracks I remembered it now it felt like a lifetime ago. "I take it you remember me now, I'm here to give you your choice's again, like before.
You can die and come with me to Alicade and leave all of your family and friends behind or go back and defeat Annadora?" he asked just standing there as if it was a simple question he has just asked.
"I remember last time you gave me the option to go back and forget everything?" little snippets of the conversation were coming back to me, "that was true, you were under the age of 16 then," said Aires with a serious face.
"I don't want to fight anyone," I said shaking my head. Then all of sudden the penny dropped, Annadora was the evil fairy in one of the story's my Dad told me, surely it can't be the same one though.
He has always said it is a true story "Annadora, my Dad told me about her in a story he always used to tell me, she's an evil fairy that controls the water".
I said sitting on the floor as the realization of my choices started to become real. "She's a little more than that, she's an avatar just like you," Aires said as a matter of fact while standing over me, I looked up at him like he just escaped from the funny farm "I'm a what?" I said in a high-pitched tone.
"You're a very powerful avatar Felix, you are the one that's

going to defeat Annadora its been foreseen. You will defeat her" he said with a serious look on his face.
"How? I don't even know who she is let alone defeat her, and what do you mean by defeat her? you mean kill her?" I said believing it was true, it must be so many weird things have happened recently.
I put my hands over my face in disbelief, Aires put his hand on the top of my head calmly and said, "it's your choice, no one but you can choose you could stay or go on a quest to kill Annadora". I couldn't help the tears that were now rolling down my face.
"I want to go back, tell me how to defeat her?" I was certain that I could with a little guidance he could give me. "Felix, this is going to be very dangerous are you 100% sure you want to do this?" I stood up and wiped the last of my tears from my face "well you have told me that it's foreseen that I do it, so just tell me what to do?" I asked with desperation in my tone.
"Ok, how many powers do you have?" he questioned, "powers? do you mean the wind thing?" I asked while looking at my hands. "anything else?" he asked, I just shook my head.
"Show me how you can control the wind?" Aires asked while moving to the wall on his right side. I revealed to him what I can do which wasn't very much apparently by the look on his face.
"Felix you are a powerful avatar the wind is within you, as long as you have breath in your lungs you just need to concentrate, you need to focus all your emotions on it. When you get distracted you lose your concentration, a lot of avatars have something they hold close to them.
For me it's my farther ring" Aries said pulling the ring out of his toga, it looked like a plain gold band "will this do?" I

said while pulling out of my trouser pocket a small blood red crystal with a clear crystal running through it from top to bottom front to back, so you could just about see threw it. "Felix, where did you get that?" Aires asked taking a step back, so his back was against the wall. "

My Great Granddad gave it to me when I was like 6, he told me to always keep it with me at all times, why?" I asked.

"Did he tell you what it was?" he asked with a shaky voice, "no, why what is it?" I asked rolling it threw my fingers "Felix that's Annadora's, that's probably why we haven't seen her in a while."

Aires said and began to walk to the other side of the room, the light started again and became bright like before when he arrived "Aires wait! what do I do now?" I shouted but he was gone.

It felt like hours had passed, I sat the opposite corner staring where the light had disappeared praying for it to return but no luck.

I now have my knees pulled up with my arms wrapped around them with my face resting on my knees, I just couldn't take my eyes from the corner incase I missed something, all of a sudden, the light appeared. It started small becoming bigger, it stung my eyes like before.

I quickly got to my feet shielding my eyes and called "Aires?" in a desperate tone, "no" I recognized the voice that replied after the light dimmed I could see who it was. OMG, It was my Great Granddad Felix he doesn't look like he's aged a day since he died.

Iit was nearly 9 years ago. (Guess who I was named after) he was wearing the same kind of toga as Aires but he was white, not grey, ok let me tell you something about my Great Granddad he was 93 years old when he died but he looked much younger than before he passed, he looked like an older version of my Dad but with Grey hair. "Granddad Felix, what

the hell is going on? Aires says I'm some sort of powerful avatar and I need to defeat someone called Annadora" I said. "Felix it's all true, you are a very powerful avatar even more powerful than myself," he said putting his hands on my shoulders to try and calm me down.
"Please explain it to me as I don't understand, why do I have these powers but Red, Ben, and Freddy don't have them and I'm pretty sure Dad's not got them either" I said in an annoyed tone, I was starting to get worked up again "I cannot tell you why only a few of us have them, no one really knows why it skipped generations. Felix, it's a precious gift you need to protect it" he said while trying to calm me down. He was still holding my shoulders, but his hold wasn't so strong.
"Ok tell me how it works and how do I defeat Annadora?", over the next few hours, Granddad Felix told me all he knew about Annadora and that she only has one weakness ‹the crystal› that was firmly back in my pocket and it was not leaving my presence.
"So, this crystal of hers, what is it?" I asked as we walked around the room again "I will try to explain it so you will understand, most of the avatars only possess one power but a few can possess two.
It's very rare to have two, the more powerful ones get given a crystal called the Crybecker. It gives that person the ability to possess the other elements.
In my case I can control the earth element then I got given my Crybecker and now I can control all of them" my Granddad Felix said while showing me his Crybecker that he just pulled out of his toga.
It was a lot smaller than Annadora's, it was blue with a little half-moon on it, "so, because I can control the wind I will get a Crybecker thing as well" I asked still looking down

at the Crybecker in his hands.
"No not all the avatars will get them, but you don't need one, let's just say your different Felix". "What do you mean by different?" I asked looking up at him, "what I mean is how you possess the power, you have to die by that specific power. Just like when you were 9 the wind blows the tree over and you come here to train your powers with Aires, how did you die this time Felix?".
"I drowned," I said in disbelief shaking my head, "Felix" I heard so faintly as though it was a whisper.
I looked around to see where the female voice came from, "Granddad Felix did you hear that?" I asked thinking I was going mad. "Hear what?" he asked while looking over his shoulder "it sounded like someone saying my name "Felix" there did you hear it just then?", I felt a little jumpy now.
I heard it for the third time, very faint, I'm sure they are calling my name, "yes I can hear it but it doesn't sound like your Mother it sounds younger" he said while looking at me waiting for me to reply. Its Star, it must be "Star" I shouted, "who's Star, Felix?" "Star Redfield, she just moved in next door, before I came here I was attacked in my garden and she started defending me she fought with the man who attacked. I can't think what she called him" I said putting my hands over my face to try and remember the name, "Kayos," I said out loud "Yes" he replied as though he knew who I was talking about.
"How did you know that?" I asked so confused with this whole situation, "his name is Kayos Redfield son to Annadora, brother to Star and Chadwick Redfield. They are very dangerous Felix you need to stay away from them, please tell me you will" he was now looking at me with a serious face, I had never seen him look at anyone like this before.

I took a step back trying to get my head around what he has just told me 'Star is the daughter of the woman I need to kill it can't be true, it must be a mistake'.
"Kayos was in my room he must have been looking for something, Star is different, she's not evil, she's not," I said in a demanding tone.
"They are only after one thing Felix, the crystal and nothing else," said Granddad Felix as a matter of fact.
I dropped down to the floor feeling light-headed, the room started to spin "what's going on? I feel dizzy" I whispered holding my hands out trying to steady myself.
"You're going back to your body Felix" he said while putting a hand on my back, "no I'm not ready to go, I need to know how to defeat her, you need to help me" but by the time I had finished my sentence I felt like I was falling and falling fast.
Suddenly, I hit the floor with a massive bump and my eyes flew open taking a huge gulp of air that hurt my lungs that hurt so bad I thought my chest was going to explode.

# CHAPTER 10

I could see Star kneeling over me and she was crying uncontrollably, Karl was freaking out behind her and Sean was doing CPR chatting to himself "not again, you're not doing this to me again".

"Felix," Sean said aloud with so much relief in his voice, it made me feel bad being away for so long. "Sean stop pushing on my chest" I squeezed out "sorry mate," he said holding up his hands "oh Felix," Star said falling forward and hugging me so tight I couldn't breathe again.

I could still see Karl freaking out if I remember correctly he mega freaked out the last time and had to go to a physiotherapist twice a week for three years.

'I will need to explain this to him as soon as possible' I thought.

My eyes began to focus on the pool over Stars shoulder "why is the pool bubbling like that?" I asked it looked weird I've never seen it do that before.

I tried to get up, but Star still had me in a bear hug "it's been doing it for about five minutes, since Star pulled you out of the pool" whispered Karl, I could see he was trying to calm himself down, but he was starting to shake, "I've only been gone five minutes?" I said quietly.

"I thought I lost you" Star whispered squeezed a little tighter then let go, it felt so nice her skin was so soft, I didn't ever want her to let go.

I noticed her hair was starting to shift colour from dark brown to a lighter brown 'I really need to ask her about that at some point but first I need to help Karl and explain to him' I thought "help me up and let's go inside and I will try and explain what happened" I said as I was putting my hand out to be pulled up.

Once upstairs I checked in my parent's room, no sign of them so I then looked in Freddy's room and there was my Mum fast asleep on Freddy's bed. She was curled up with him, they looked so comfortable.

But still no sign of my Dad he wasn't downstairs when we come in 'he must still be next door with Calvin' I thought while walking into my room and closing the door behind me. Karl was sitting on my bed shaking his head and now biting his nails, Star was sitting on the floor in the corner and Sean was sitting on my computer chair with his arms across his chest.

"Go on explain, we are all ears" Sean said in an annoyed tone "I don't know where to start, I can only assume that when my heart stopped beating my spirit was transported, all I can remember was opening my eyes and seeing white walls, the room didn't have anything in it.

I was alone for what felt like a long time then Aires turned up like last time something like this happened, but I couldn't remember at the time as I was too young to make the choice.

He told me what I really am, it's not aerokinesis like you thought it was, I'm an avatar and a very powerful one at that apparently" I said while looking into Sean's eyes.

"I think you're trying to pull a fast one," said Sean getting angry, "please listen, Sean, for Karl's sake he needs to know fully what's going on.

You don't want him to go back to that useless doctor?" I

said raising my voice as I felt a little annoyed that he didn't believe me.
"No, you were saying you're an avatar" said Sean unfolding his arms like he was now ready to listen to me, "Aires gave me a choice either I die and go with him to Alicade or come back and defeat someone" I said looking over at Star, she was looking up at the ceiling.
"So did this Aires tell you who it was?" asked Sean "err yes its someone called Annadora" Star put her hands over her eyes, "Annadora the fairy Queen she's evil, she went on a murderous rampage when something got stolen from her?" said Karl. He had stopped biting his nails so I kind of take it he's not freaking out anymore now he knows what's going on, he is now listening to what transpired.
"I think we should talk about that another time but I'm not finished, my Great Granddad Felix was there too, he was an avatar as well and he told me that most avatars only possess one or two of the element powers and the more powerful ones are given a Crybecker to possess the others elements but I won't get one as I'm like a Crybecker.
I am the power, the power is in me I possess them all but there's one little snag. I have to die by the element, like when I was 9 and the wind blew me out of the tree and I died, same as today, I just drowned and now I possess the water element now" the room fell silent.
They all were staring at me, suddenly I heard laughing coming from behind me. All four of us looked at the door, it was the Satan twins laughing as they fell in the door.
They were laughing so hard they fell to the floor holding their stomachs "what the hell are you talking about dying and possessing powers? I think you need to go to a special place with padded walls" Red said trying to catch his breath.
"Yeah and take your freaky friends with you" Ben added.

I was fuming 'I will show them' I thought while putting my left arm out with my palm facing them, they carried on laughing. I made the motion of slamming a door with my left hand and the door slammed closed they soon stopped and got to their feet, they just stood there huddled together, I could see both of their faces turning white.
"What the!" Red said trying to open the door, I put both arms out palms facing up to the ceiling and I started to lift them both off the floor. As my hands got higher so did they until they were lying flat on their backs on the ceiling.
"Put us down Felix" shouted Ben panicking "yeah come on bro put us down," said Red as though it now didn't bother him.
So, I did as they asked, I put them down. I probably should have done it a bit slower, but they needed to be taught a lesson not to mess with me anymore, don't get me wrong I didn't let them slam to the floor but they were dam close.
"Believe me now?" I asked putting my arms down beside me, they quickly scrabbled to their feet "how can you do that? can we do it too?" asked Red putting his arms out and trying to copy my previous actions.
"No, you can't it's just me and Granddad Felix he was an avatar too but not as strong as me. No one has seen any one as powerful as me apparently, they can't explain it" I said shaking my head.
"There's been one other," Star said whispering tears now flowing freely from her eyes "what do you mean?" I asked walking closer to her "there was one other called Baltazar, he is the first avatar where all others were made, you are called a mod avatar" Star said standing up "why didn't Aires tell me or my Great Granddad Felix? how do you know? and they mustn't?" I said, in a questionable tone.
"It was told as a bedtime story, read to me by my Mother,"

Star said looking into my eyes knowing that I would understand.
“Your Mother Anna?” Star just nodded at me as though she was looking through me.
“Wonderful, just wonderful, I don’t need to know this right now, we just need to know how am I going to go about getting my last two powers, fire, and earth? any ideas?”.
“Well fire will be easy, we can set you alight,” said Karl with a grin on his face “well that sounds painful and what about earth?” I said with a shiver running down my back
“Buried alive!” said Red.
“Great I’m going to be burnt to the stake then buried alive, just another ordinary weekend for me then,” I said in a sarcastic tone while sitting on my bed.
“It’s ok Felix we will help you get through it,” said Karl patting me on the back.
“Thanks mate but I can’t ask you to help it’s too much” ‘they could seriously get hurt’ I thought to myself.
“We are with you if you like it or not,” said Sean standing up, he walked over to Ben and Red and pushed them towards me.
“We all are Ent we,” he said “if we get to kill you without actually killing you we are so in” they looked way too excited.
“Well, it’s getting late I better be going,” Star said putting her hands on my shoulders “I will walk you out,” I said getting up off my bed, when Star was leaving the room Red and Ben started making kissing noises.
OK, OK I know I probably shouldn’t have done what I did, I quickly turned around and throw my arms out and the wind pushed Red and Ben across the room.
I quickly left the room and closed the door, once outside Star pulled me down the side of the house so no one could see us, “Star I understand if you don’t want to help me as it is

your Mother that I have to defeat and......." Star put her hands up to stop me.

"Felix I'm in, it's just my Dad told me not to get involved with you and I can see why now but I just can't stay away from you it's like I'm pulled to you.

All I ask is that you please don't tell the others that Annadora is my Mother, I just don't want them to think I'm just like her" Star said taking a step back.

"I won't tell, so now that we are alone I think we need to talk about some things" I said in a hushed tone.

"Shoot" she said as though she was all ears, "I don't know how to say this without sounding stupid but why does your hair change colour?" I asked while looking at the ends of her hair.

"So, you noticed it then, well I'm a daughter of an avatar that is also a fairy and my Dad is wizard and human so..." Star shrugged her shoulders.

"Wow, so you're like a hybrid? well at least I'm not the only freak around here" I laughed so loud, Star hit me on the arm and said, "we are not freak's we are...... special".

That was it we were both laughing "so does it change with your mood?" I said flicking her hair "no, it changes with how much power I have, so when the sun goes down I draw it in, that's the reason why it changes but when I touch you I feel the same type of charge" she said trying to explain why it happens.

"So, what does it feels like?" I asked leaning my back against the wall "it feels like pins and needles in my fingers, what about you? what does it feel like controlling the elements?".

"I can only control two of them but it's weird as I know it's not natural, but it feels right does that make sense? when I control the air, it feels like the air is rushing through my veins" I said while holding up my arms.

“Felix is that you?” called Dad “yeah” I shouted back. I turned to Star and rolled my eyes “hi Mr. Moon” Star said, Dad was closer to us now he had just walked around the corner. “Ah Star my dear your Father is looking for you, he tried to call you a few times while I was there,” he said while looking a little concerned. “Oh, I kind of dropped my phone in the pool earlier” Star quickly glanced at me as I knew the truth, I knew she saved me.

“Well then, I better be going, see you tomorrow Felix,” Star said touching my arm and walking off, once she was behind Dad she turned and wiggled her fingers at me, I smiled as I knew that she felt the charge I just gave her by the slight touch.

“Come on son, so did you have a good birthday?” he asked while swinging his arm over my shoulder “let’s just say it was eventful”.

# CHAPTER 11

While walking back in my room I noticed Red and Ben had left, Sean was on my computer typing away and Karl was fiddling with my new phone while lying on his tummy on my bed. “what are you two doing?” I asked as if nothing had happened.

“Well me and Karl were talking while you were gone, as we don’t know much about avatars were looking it up, so we can be more useful to you,” Sean said while concentrating on my computer screen.

“Here listen to this” Karl said while moving in to the sitting position, after I had sat down next to him and Sean moved to sit the other side he began to read from my phone screen “an avatar is a name they give someone who can bend the elements” he said looking up from the phone “we already know this” Sean said butting in “yes but did you know there are five powers, not four” he said with excitement in his voice.

“what? no there’s only four, wind, water, earth and fire, one, two, three, four.” I said counting them out using my fingers.

“This says there is an extra one they call it energy bending, energy bending is the ability to take away someone’s power e.g. energy, powers, bending abilities or to restore energy e.g. energy, powers, bending ability, it’s very, very rare,” Karl said.

"No way let me read that," Sean said taking the phone from Karl and taking it back over to the computer. "You know what, I think I've already got that power," I said while looking over Sean's shoulder, "why do you think that?" Karl asked. "Well isn't all avatars born with one power? I died by wind and water to get them powers when I walked Star outside and I found out that she has a mix of magical things a hybrid of sorts and you know I told you about her hair changing colour? well it usually only changes with power from a setting sun but when she touches me she gets the same kind of charge" I tried to explain to them both, although it does sound kind of stupid.

"Wow this is getting so crazy right now I think I need a break," Karl said getting up off the bed and started pacing the room. "Ok, no more avatar talks for the rest of the night," I said putting my hands-on Karl's shoulders to try and calm him down, it worked a little bit, so for the rest of the night, me and Karl played some video games as Sean refused to get off the computer.

In the morning I woke up with a jerk as someone sat on my bed "Star, how...how did you get in?" I asked trying to pull the bed covers over my nacked chest.

"Your Mum let me in," she said scanning my body "Ok then how did you get into my room as the door was locked from the inside?" I asked, "a hybrid remember," Star said pointing to herself being all proud.

I just laughed while scooting my butt up, so I could lean my back against the headboard on my bed. Star scooted up next to me and said in a low tone, "that can't be comf ortable?" Star nodded over at Sean, he was still in the computer chair his feet were up on the computer table and leaning so far back in the chair it was on the verge of tipping back.

"He is so going to fall" I laughed "that's mean, come on help me make him feel more comfortable," Star said while smiling. I started to move too so I could get up off the bed when she pulled on my shoulder "no, try using your powers, try lifting him up out of the chair".

"Ok" 'I could do this' I thought to myself, so I closed my eyes and let the air fill my head, I put my arms out and started lifting but the chair was coming up as well. So, I put it back down gently "concentrate on him not the chair" Star whispered.

I just nodded and tried again this time the chair stayed where it was, and I lifted just Sean a good four feet of the chair "Star where am I going to put him?" I asked not worried I was going to drop him.

Star got off the bed and stood back "put him here" she said while pointing at the now empty space she had just moved from.

So, I slowly got out of the bed keeping all of my concentration on Sean and moved him towards the bed, once he was over the bed I stared lowering him down, I caught a glimpse of Star smiling and I lost it and dropped him it wasn't that far, his body just bounced on the bed but it didn't wake him up.

"That was close," Star said taking her hands away from her mouth. I walked over to by draws and pulled out a t-shirt and jogging bottoms, "I'm getting good at that!" I said over my shoulder we both just laughed.

I got changed in the bathroom and brushed my teeth and hair, "what you doing in there? you take longer than a girl" Star said, I could hear her laughing behind the door.

While walking out of the bathroom I couldn't help saying "it takes time for perfection" with a massive grin on my face.

We went downstairs and walked into the kitchen "morning

Mum, mini me" I said to Freddy ruffling his hair, "fix, fix, fix" Freddy said jumping up at me, he can't quit saying Felix yet but it's better than him calling me, Fifi.
So, I picked him up and he played with my hair my body humming with every little twist of my hair.
"Oh, what have you got for breakfast little man? Mm, lucky charms, my favorite" I said lifting a spoon full and putting it in my mouth, Freddy quickly struggled to get down, he quickly sat at the table and started eating his cereal "Felix where's Sean and Karl? they not hungry?" Mum asked.
"They're still asleep" I replied "oh ok would you like your breakfast now or wait for them to wake? Star would you like some too?" Mum asked.
"That would be nice Mrs. Moon," Star said with a shy smile on her face, "please call me Sue, what would you like to eat?" she asked while pottering around in the kitchen.
"Anything I'm not fussy" Star replied.
After we both ate our amazing cooked breakfast of 'bacon, sausages, and eggs mmm I could eat it again I thought to myself' me and Star went in the back garden.
"A lot has happened in the last 12 hours," Star said while scanning the garden "you can say that again" I replied. We stopped by the pool and you could see a dent where my head had hit the concentrate, if that was anyone else I'm sure it would have split their head open! "you know what that really hurt, that man was an idiot" I said while rubbing my head, "that was my brother Kayos.
Let's just say that was mild" she said now looking at me "oh god I don't know if I can do this" I said walking away from the pool, I turned and picked up a chair that looked as though it had been thrown on the floor, after putting it upright I sat down.
"Yes, you can Felix we are going to help you," she said while

walking towards another chair dumped on the grass.
"How Star? how are they going to help me? Huh? they aren't human, I've only got two powers" "three" Star interrupted.
"So, the energy one is true then?" I asked while looking at the tips of her hair "yes, I spoke to my Father and he confirmed it, I thought you would of already know about that one as your helping Freddy and me" all I heard was the name Freddy, I got up so fast and grabbed Stars arm I didn't realize how tight I had grabbed it until I could see the pain in her eyes.
"What about Freddy?" I asked in a pissed off tone "ouch Felix" Star said with a shocked look on her face.
"Sorry, what do you mean by helping Freddy?" I asked while letting go of her arm, "Freddy is sick" she said with a worried look on her face.
I couldn't help sitting down on the chair with a bump I felt that the life was being drawn from me.
"What do you mean he's sick?" I said trying to calm myself.
"Freddy has leukemia," she said in a low voice as though she didn't want anyone else to overhear.
"What, but how? why?" I couldn't understand it "I can't say how or why but he has," she said as though she was telling me 2 x 2 was 4.
"How do you know?" I asked, I have to admit I started crying like a baby, I couldn't help but sob he was my baby brother, he was ill and I didn't even know. So many things went through my head, 'does Mum and Dad know? was he receiving treatment without us all knowing'?
Star keeled down and put her hands on my shoulders "it's the fairy part of me, but you are helping him, FELIX ARE YOU LISTENING TO ME," Star shook me "yes" I whispered "you are the one that's fighting it without knowing it.
You know about the energy power, that's what's helping him.

You know he runs his fingers throw your hair that's where he feels the 'charge', but every little touch helps him, like when you hold him so don't be sad" Star hugged me until I felt calmer, "get a room" Sean shouted, and Karl laughed while eating some toast.
Star let me go "oh god what's the matter Felix?" said Sean quickly running around the pool to where I was sitting.
I filled them in on Freddy and they were shocked, they both promised to keep it secret, another one to add to the list.
The Satan twins just joined us, so we changed the subject and started talking about how I'm going to get my other two powers, "I think you should leave that with us" said Red with a huge grin on his face.
"Yes, I think we will be best people for that job" Ben added.
"Great my life or should I say my death is in your hands but I'm thinking we should do this in the summer holidays, so we have three weeks to prepare". They all nodded their heads to show they all agreed.
So, for the three weeks running up to the summer holidays me and Star practiced on my bending abilities, now I can throw water like it's a ball or hold it up like a barrier and push the wind but not at the same time.
I was getting good, like really good. I was spending all my free time with Freddy, the best time is at night when he comes into my room and I lay on the bed with him and let him play with my hair watching the lights dance around my room.
Once he falls asleep I can't bear to put him to bed so I let him sleep in with me and I always try to keep my hand on his so there's always contact between us.
For the last week before the school holiday Star had been coming to my room at night once Freddy had fallen asleep, she didn't want to freak him out.

She would just appear with no warning, Star was standing at the window in red jogging bottoms a jacket and a bright pink scarf wrapped around her neck, the tips of her hair were blond.
'She must have charged herself up as they were black this morning' I thought to myself, "how is he today?" I ask Star the same question every day as soon as she appears in my room, she must get so fed-up with me asking.
"He is getting better, I think it's in remission, Felix you are doing a good job you need to be proud of yourself," she said.
"What does remission mean?" I asked I felt so drained, "well its difficult as its still there but it's a lot smaller than before, I would say another week maybe two and it would be gone" Star said now sitting on the side of the bed next to where Freddy was sound asleep, I was still touching his hand, every bit of energy will help him.
"Are you ready to train some more?" she asked looking up at me, I inhaled a deep breath and closed my eyes, I know I should train but I don't want to leave Freddy, I exhaled and just nodded.
In a flash we went from my room to Drake Forest, Drake Forest is private, very private as no one in their right mind would come in the forest after dark as its scary as hell.
We worked on some defense tactics, Star would charge at me and I had to stop her, I pushed her away that hard she slammed into a tree making it crack "oh god Star, I'm so sorry" I said rushing up to her but she wasn't there she had disappeared, then I heard a whistle from behind me "Star" I spun around but she wasn't there neither "STAR" I shouted, then there was another whistle "Star where are you? It's not funny" I called out.
"Come find me" Star called, it sounded like she was to the left of me, so I started slowly walking that way, "come on, I

don't have your freaky hybrid powers" I shouted getting a little annoyed.
"Ouch, now that's not nice" all of a sudden, I went flying, she had bloody pushed me over, I didn't even see her behind me. I fell, and I fell hard "now who's not being nice," I said getting up on my feet and brushing the dirt off my trousers, "Felix you control the energy power you should have been able to sense the energy change in your surroundings? close your eyes" she said while walking towards me.
So, I did as instructed, she pulled her scarf from around her neck and wrapped it around my head so my eyes were covered, I couldn't see a damn thing through it.
"Don't you think this is a little bit over the top? does it look good on me?" I said standing in a posing position by putting my hands on my hips and tilted my head up to the right, "very groovy, now just feel, don't think about anything just feel.
Now I'm going to move and you're going to turn to the direction I'm in and you tell me if I'm near or far away, got it?" Star asked while walking away from me, "I've got it" I said nodding "starting...... now".
I tried to hear where she was but all I heard was the breeze hitting the leaves on the trees or the occasional owl hooting "ok, no thinking, just feeling" I whispered to myself then I started getting a funny tingling on my right side, I slowly turned to the right I could feel the tingling was there growing stronger. I slowly walked forward until it stopped, I put my hand out and said, "you're there".
"Well done how far away do you think I am?" she said faintly, "I don't know three miles away?" I replied jokingly "not funny again".
For the next hour and a half, this is what we focused our training on, I fingered out that the stronger the tingles were

the closer Star was and the faint tingles meant she was far away.

"It's getting late I think we should call it a night," Star said while taking off my blind fold, "your hair is changed colour?" I said picking up some of her hair.

"It's all the jumping around I've been doing its draining, do you mind if I charge?" she said while putting her hand on my arm.

"I'm not a plug socket, but it's fine" I laughed, Star punched my shoulder with her other hand and then held it. "So how long do you think it would take to charge up this way?" I asked, to be honest, I loved holding her hand I didn't want it to ever stop "I don't know I've never done this before" she replied, we began to walk around for a while talking about Annadora and why she turned evil.

"She hasn't always been bad but when she met my Dad she cleaned herself up, she had Kayos, Chadwick and me, she was a bit of a rebel when she was younger but when her sister was killed she fell off the wagon so to speak and that's where your Great Granddad Felix comes in.

He took something from her and she lost the plot killing as many avatars as she could" She said as if she was saying I had two heads.

Annadora's Crybecker now felt like a lead weight in my pocket "so is all of your family ‹special›" I asked looking at her, "well you know I›m ‹special› so is Kayos, he has had more time to perfect his ability, my Mum is an avatar/fairy and my Dad is a witch/human, Chadwick had the ability of foresight but there was an accident when he was younger and he lost it" just the thought of Kayos made me put my spare hand up to my chest remembering the pain.

"So, what do the colours in your hair mean?" I questioned trying to change the subject off Annadora, "black means

normal power, enough for me to do little jumps like from my room to yours, brown is half charge and blond if full power" she said while running her hand through her hair.
"What about red?" I said flicking her hair, Star quickly let go of my hand "red is bad, it's too much power for me I can't handle it" she said with a worried look on her face "Star calm down you're fine" I said while grabbing her hand back "we need to go" she said.
Before I could say 'but' we were back in my room "bye Felix" Star kissed me on the cheek then left. "What was that all about," I said shrugging my shoulders.
Freddy was still in my bed when I returned, so I got my PJ's on and laid next to him, he stirred a little so I cuddled up to him until I could feel the humming, I fell into a peaceful sleep.

# CHAPTER 12

"Wake up sleepy head it's your last day of school," said Mum while picking Freddy up off my bed. I got up and looked at myself in the mirror "this is going to be a long summer".

The last day of school went in a blur, once back at home I sat on the sofa with my head in my hands, "Felix, Felix, Felix" Red and Ben said together "we have figured everything out. We know how to kill you, in a good way" said Ben "I don't want to hear all this right now" I said while raising my head to look at them both.

"Sean and Karl will be here soon and then we will talk about it" "the sooner we do this the sooner you get the power," Red said.

"Fix, fix" Freddy screamed while bouncing in the room "shhh later, hey mini-me, what you been up to?" I asked as the Satan twins left the room, Freddy and I watched some cartoons together until Sean and Karl turned up just after 6, We all went to my room to talk in private. "When are we going to do this?" I said pacing my room.

"What have Ben and Red got?" asked Karl, "let's just say their ready to go at any time".

"Where's Star?" "right here," Star said right behind me, "what the...! you scared the hell out of me," I said while looking over my shoulder.

"Sorry, I just thought you were used to it by now," Star said while laughing and tapping my shoulder. I grabbed her before she walked off "are you ok after last night?", "fine, I will explain later".

I let go of her arm and she sat next Karl putting one arm over his shoulder.

So, we decided on the, how do you say it, the killing of me, my power possession, the insanity they call my life, it was going to happen two weeks Saturday which gives me enough time with Freddy.

"So, two weeks time me and Karl will be staying around here," said Sean, I just nodded.

For the rest of the night, we did normal teenage stuff like talking, joking around and play games, eating all the food we could find, I even spoke to Star when the other two was playing their turn on the Xbox.

"So why were you so freaked out yesterday when your hair went red?" I asked while laying down on my bed, she was sitting upright next to me "Red is bad", "you said it was too much power for you I would have thought the more power you have the stronger you are?" "it is but when my Mum tried to turn us, she always made me have so much power and it's addictive having all that power flowing through you, I nearly went with her, I loved the power and now I can't handle it. I don't want it to take over me so it's a no-go area."

"You're such a cheater Sean, I won that game," Karl said punching him in the arm. "Come on children, play nice" I laughed "Sean cheated he keeps using the cheat roads". "There called short cuts and they are there for that reason", "he's got a point there Karl".

"Best out of three?" Sean just nodded, and they began playing again.

For the remainder of the night me and Star just stayed on the bed talking, Sean and Karl left mine just after 10.
The first week flu past, getting the details ready for my death/power possession all in to place, it was all going down at Drake Forest, Karl didn't like the idea of going back there but it's the best place, out the way so no one will see but close enough if anything goes wrong.
The Satan twins were extremely excited, more than they probably should be about killing me.
The second week went much slower, much, much slower, I just stayed with Freddy most of the time.
On Thursday I asked Star the same question as always about Freddy and she told me he was showing as being all clear, I honestly think that this moment was the happiest point in my life.
Freddy means everything to me and Star knows that when she told me I jumped off my bed (carefully as not to wake Freddy) and hugged her so tight. "I. Cant. Breath" Star struggled to say, "sorry, is he really all clear?" I said still with my arms around her but not as tight.
"Yes it's all gone, he might be a little weak for a few days but other than that he's all good", "god I'm so happy," I said with tears in my eyes.
"Freddy is all better and it's all because of you, your training is top notch and you will have your next power shortly, you're doing excellent Felix," Star said putting her hands on either side of my face and looking deep into my Grey eyes.
In the corner of my eye, I noticed that Stars hair was turning red, so I quickly stepped back letting her go "your, err hair is turning red" I said while pointing at her hair.
"Oh, right thank you, are you ready for your penultimate day of training?" "yeah, what are we training on tonight?"

“balance” I just looked confused, I stood on one leg “what like this?” “no, you idiot, the balance between the powers, the balance of using more than one power at a time,” Star said holding up her hand level pointing towards me.
“Sounds interesting, let’s go,” I said holding out my hand to touch hers and then we were gone.
It was D-day, the day of the fire possession, I won’t lie to you I was scared like really scared.
We all thought it would be best if Karl didn’t come to the actual event as we all knew he wouldn’t  cope very well, he agreed to stay at my house but on one condition that he was updated every five minutes which Sean agreed to.
I didn’t really want anyone there, but I knew I couldn’t do it alone.
That night I got Freddy to sleep while Star and Karl waited for me, once asleep I took Freddy to his own bed. While leaving his room I got caught by my Mum “hey Felix love, what are you up to? not having Freddy in bed with you tonight?” she asked.
It must have looked strange for the past few weeks he has slept with me, so I can give him as much charge as he needed.
“No not tonight, his all better now” I mistakenly said, “what do you mean better?” She quizzed. “Oh, he said he had a belly ache” it was the first thing that popped in to my head, what could I say, I have been healing your son with my powers, I would sound crazy! “oh, ok thank you, Felix, goodnight” “goodnight Mum” then she turned to walk away. “Mum, I love you, I just wanted you to know that” “oh Felix I love you too, what bought all this on? do you want to talk?”. “It’s nothing, it’s just I don’t think I say it enough to you and Dad, goodnight” “goodnight love”.
I nearly ran back to my room I was so close to crying in front

of my Mum and if I did I would have told her everything, it would have all came out of me in a slobbery mess.
I closed the door and lent back on it putting my hands over my face "are you ok Felix?" Star asked making me jump once again.
I had forgotten that she was still waiting in my room "I'm fine I just need a minute" "take all the time you need, do you want me to leave?".
"No, I will be fine, where's Karl?" "shower, he didn't want to be here when you go" I just nodded and took a few deep breaths "I'm ready to die" and we were gone.
At the 'site' there was a little fire going, a metal funnel above it catching the smoke that led to a 4-foot-high wooden box with smoke seeping out the gaps, the plan was for me to die by smoke inhalation instead of actually being set on fire.
"So, all I do is get in the box?" "Yeah, get in the box and die, basally," said Red.
"Then that's where I come in, I can sense when you die, sorry pass away, we take you out the box leave you for two minutes before Sean performs CPR just like before when you drowned" "why two minutes?" I questioned.
"Because your brain will start to be starved of oxygen, the sooner we bring you back the better chance you will get of coming back" "how do we know this is going to work?" I asked staring at the box of doom "you remember when the wind blew you out of the tree".
"Yes, it's something you don't really forget" I said, "we have come to the conclusion that the fall from the tree killed you not the wind its self so we think that the smoke from the fire will do the same" said Sean pointing at the box "but you're not 100% sure, so this could kill me, like really kill me".
"No one knows how this works Felix there's not a text book

for this sort of stuff," Star said, after taking a few more deep breaths I said, "let's do this".
I got in the box as planned, I'm going to spare you all the details, but it wasn't pleasant, they must have put something on the fire as the smoke turned from thin white smoke to thick heavy black smoke all of a sudden, I was back in the white room.

# CHAPTER 13

"ARIES, GRANDDAD FELIX, SHOW YOURSELF NOW" I shouted knowing I only had two to five minutes in the 'real' world which meant I had about 12 hours here. I need to find out as much as I can about me having five powers and not four like they think and about Baltazar, "dear Felix why all the shouting?" Aires appeared, he didn't have a white light as before.

"I need answers and I need them now, why didn't you tell me about the fifth power?" "what fifth power?" he questioned.

"Don't play dumb with me Aires I know about the energy power and about Baltazar", I didn't know about him, but it sounded good so I just went with it, Aires mouth dropped at the mention of Baltazar's name "how... how do you know about him?" he said in a shaking tone.

"This is not how this works, you want me to defeat Annadora, I ask the questions and I want you to tell me everything right now," I said pointing at him.

He hesitated for a minuet before replying "we always knew that you were the chosen one from when you were born, nearly killed your mother at birth by taking her energy from her, your Great Grandfather informed us. We have been watching over you ever since" "well you have done a crappy job, what about Baltazar?" I said shocked with the revelation about my Mum, but I was on a mission and nothing was going to derail me not now I've come too far. "No one talks about him," Aires said pacing back and forth "well you're going to break your silence now, who is he?" I said while sitting on the floor.

"Baltazar was the first avatar that we were all made from" "what do you mean by that? I thought it was a freak of nature not man-made".

"The first ones were 'man-made' as you put it, there were about 5000 of us made from all walks of life, human, witch, fairy, werewolves, vampires you name it there's an avatar". 'Note to self-tell Sean and Karl everything they believe in is real', "so all the first ones made are all full avatar like me?" "no Baltazar was very cunning he only gave one power to us all and a Crybecker to the stronger ones, but he was still more powerful as he had the energy power". "But why wouldn't you tell me this it's the history of the avatars?" I said still not understanding why he wouldn't tell me "Baltazar wanted to be god, he wanted everyone to bow down to him and the ones that wouldn't he would kill, a handful of us ran and we worked to over throw him, the witches and warlocks bound him with black magic and the vampires drained him of blood but he wouldn't die we tried all sorts to try to kill him but to no avail, so he was chained and buried in a secret location".

'Lake Halo' popped in my head as that was where Great Granddad Felix would go fishing at least twice a month and where the whole family would go on weekend holidays all the time.

"So, what happens now?" I said shrugging my shoulders not letting on that I think I know where he is "now we train, what element do you have possession of?" Aires asked holding his hand out "fire" I said taking his hand, he pulled

me to my feet.
"Ok fire is the hardest to master as the human body does not have fire in it, fire needs lots of concentration".
Most of the training was me sitting on the floor with my eyes closed concentrating trying to light a fire when I click my fingers, but I failed "come on Felix concentrate" "what do you think I'm doing, sitting here clicking my fingers for the fun of it?" "that's exactly what it looks like" I felt my blood boil I was mad as I was trying really hard "concentrate".
"I'm too angry to do it, look," I said clicking my fingers and there was the fire on the end of my thumb, flicking orange and yellow flame "wow," I said looking at the flame closer.
It was real as I could feel the heat on my face but there was no heat on my finger where the flame was dancing on my thumb "that's strange none of the other avatars can possess the power when angry" Aires said rubbing his head.
All of a sudden I heard my name being called "Felix" this time it was Sean calling me "well that's it time up for practice maybe when I come back with earth" "wait, Felix, you're not going back yet there's still too much to teach you" "well our time is up sorry" I said still hearing Sean calling for me, I started to feel the dizzy sensation start.
Aires clicked his fingers and the room turned a dark shade of Grey just like someone turned a light off and wasn't so bright and my dizziness had stopped, and I couldn't here Sean anymore.
"Aires what have you done?" "we have not finished yet" "no Aires I need to go back, I've had my time here, it's time for me to go back to the real world, so click your fingers and let me go".
"Sorry, that's not going to happen" I was getting angry again and I can feel the fire flow throw me. I clicked my fingers and ignited the flame, I didn't know how to use it, but I guessed

it was like using the others.
I rolled the flame into a ball in my hands, it's kind of freaky standing here with a ball of fire in my hands and it not even hurting,
I remembered when I was 5, I burnt my hand at a bonfire,
I still had a little scare on my left hand from it but it didn't hurt to everyone's surprise.
I pushed the ball of flames towards Aries and he puts it out with water and then he pushed me back with the air power, it was much stronger than mine, we fought like this for a short time until I remembered, even though I don't have the earth power I do have a power Aires doesn't have.
I closed my eyes just like when Star had blind folded me in the wood and I tried to remember what she said about feeling where she was.
I knew where he was as he was giving off a different vibration, I was thinking of a vacuum sucking up the dirt, but I was sucking his powers away and I could feel it in my fingers, now I know how Star feels when she touches me.
"Felix stop it" he shouted, I just ignored his plea. When the tingling stopped in my fingers I knew it was done, I opened my eyes and Aires was lying on the floor, he wasn't dead as I could see that he was breathing but I knew I had taken all his powers.
I quickly ran over to him and found his Crybecker in his pocket I quickly took it and held it to sight in my hand.
A few hours passed before Aires woke up "Felix" he said in a weary voice "I'm still here" "what happened?" "You trapped me here and we fought and I kind of won, so I took my trophy," I said rolling his Crybecker in my fingers.
"Felix give me that now" I just shook my head, Aires started to try standing up, I used the wind and blow him back down to the floor "no powers for you if you carry on, I won't give

them back, “I was sitting here thinking if I’m the same as Baltazar can I make avatars?” Aires was silent.
“Well if you want this back, start talking,” I said throwing his Crybecker in the air and making it hover there for a few seconds then letting it drop in my hand and every time I let it drop Aires flinched “so you going to tell me or not?” Aires stayed quiet, so I threw the crystal really high in the air and crossed my arms looking at him with a wicked smile on my face.
When it started to fall I could see the panic in Aires eyes “OK, OK, OK I will tell you” he finally shouted.
I stopped the Crybecker form crashing to the floor by grabbing it just in time.
It was so close to it you could just get a piece of paper between them, two at a push “so?” I questioned, “yes, you could but no one knows how as none of us can do it”.
“Good to know, now let me go back to the real world and you can have this back” Aires quickly clicked his fingers and the bright white light appeared, I started feeling dizzy like before, I placed his Crybecker on the floor next to me.
“Aires when I come back, make sure you’re not here, ensure my Great Granddad is” but before he could answer I was falling, I wasn’t panicked this time as I had been through this before and knew what was coming, I landed with a bump, all of a sudden, I was back in my body.
There was a lot less panic this time when my eyes began to open “wow that’s insane” Red said as my eyes flickered open and close trying to adjust “Felix are you ok?” asked Sean with a concerned look on his face. “Yeah I’m fine just give me a minute,” I said coughing while adjusting myself to I can sitting up.
I rubbed my hands over my face and then through my hair. I could feel the sweat and dirt in my hair and skin. Star

kneeled beside me with her head downwards, I just looked at her, I couldn't stop, I will never stop.
I could tell she had been crying "I'm fine" I whispered, "oh crap I've not told Karl what's going on," Sean said fishing his phone out of his pocket.
"Tell him we are on are way back, Star will you be able to take all of us back at once?" "it should be fine," she said touching my arm to charge herself for the journey.
Red and Ben were now trying to put the fire out that began to spread. I held my hand out towards the ground, I pulled the moisture from the wet ground, I could feel it within my body. It felt chilled as though it was running through my veins, suddenly, I blew one breath putting the fire out.
I could see the smoke coming from the grass but thankfully it had fizzled out and you could only hear the hissing.
"I don't know if I can ever get used to you doing that," Ben said shaking his head "everyone ready?" Star asked letting go of my arm and looking around.
"I think so," I said looking at everyone making sure everyone was together, they just nodded once our eyes met.
Star held my hand and everyone else just touched her other arm, two seconds later we were standing in the middle of my room.
Karl was laying on my bed reading a book with his headphones in, he didn't even notice us until Red jumped on the bed shouting "wow that was amazing" "shhh Red you fool its really late everyone is asleep do you want to explain to Mum and Dad why I'm covered in suet and smell of smoke?" "not really, but you have to admit that was cool" Red said hitting me hard in the shoulder in jest. Normally it would have hurt but since I started getting more powers and knew how to use them I have started getting stronger.
Red and Ben left the room whispering to each other, super

happy at what happened.
So, I told Sean, Karl, and Star what Aries said about me and Baltazar. They told me that I was dead for twenty minutes, I explained that Aries held me and stopped me returning, "so when are we going to do the last element?" asked Sean.
"I don't know, sooner the better but first I need a shower, we just need to talk to Red and Ben in the morning".
I walked into my bathroom, turned on the shower and began to undress, I could not wait to get in and wash the day away.
It was late when I got out of the shower, I just let the scolding hot water warm me up, walking out into my room with only my pajama bottoms on, Sean and Karl were fast asleep on the floor. Star was sitting on my window ledge looking into the room.
"I thought you had fallen asleep in there" Star joked "I don't think I can sleep after what happened I'm far too awake", all of a sudden, I remembered that I had no top, I turned my back to pull a t-shirt out of the draw when Star said "what's that?" "what's what?" "that," Star said hopping off the ledge and walking over to me, she touched between my shoulder blades like she was tracing something on my back.
"What is it?" I said turning my head to try and see it but I couldn't, "I've seen this before wait there a second" then Star was gone.
She reappeared five seconds later holding a piece of paper it looked as though it had been scrunched up but straightened out again, "Felix this is what is appearing on your back, this part" Star pointed to the three circles with the wind, fire, and water all connected with lines with a moon inside. "The bit that is missing is the sun and the leaf in a circle and these two lines".
"Star what is it?" I asked while staring at the scrunched up piece of paper, "I don't know Felix, I really don't but no other

avatar has it, so the only thing I can think of it being is the mark of the mod avatar" "great how am I going to explain that to my parents that I've got this on my back" I said while pulling a top over my head and putting my arms through the holes.

Me and Star stayed up most of the night talking until she fell asleep next to me on my bed, I still wasn›t tired I had too much to think about like why me? Why do I have to be the one that has to kill Annadora? how am I going to kill someone? let alone a woman and that woman being the Mother of the girl I really like I mean, I really like Star, where would I even find her. Yeah, I know it's been foreseen but... "CHADWICK" I said out loud while sitting bolt upright, I think I said it a little too loud as it woke everyone up "what?" Star said groggily rubbing her eyes "I need to talk to your brother" "why?" "Aries said when I was there after the water death that it has been foreseen that I have to kill Annadora but that›s all know·

I wonder if Chadwick can see the same thing" "but Felix, Chadwick lost his foresight" "I know but if I am a mod avatar then I can give back powers?" "but foresight isn't an avatar power," said Sean getting up from the floor and sitting on the end of the bed.

"I know but I do have the energy element, I'm hoping that there is some power left in him just a tiny bit that I can try and work on, do you think he will go for it?" I said looking at Star hopping that she would say 'yes, of course, he would'. "Well erm... I will ask him but when we last spoke about you he got really mad and stormed off." "But this time you can tell him that Felix could possibly give him his power back" said Karl scooting the computer chair closer to the bed, I didn't even notice that Karl was awake, "I will ask but don't hold your breath" Star said looking down at her hands that

were linked together. I put my hand on top of hers and said, "it will work Star, if he wants it bad enough he will come" she just nodded "I will ask him later, I just need to psych myself up to do it".
"Ok let's go get some breakfast I'm starving".

# CHAPTER 14

It was only just getting light outside when we went downstairs, my Mum Sue was already making breakfast "hello, your all up so early, Star I never heard you knock?" she questioned looking confused "no Mrs. Moon, Felix opened the door before I was able to".

"Ok deer well there's plenty of food to go around".

We all sat down to eat when Freddy bounced in the kitchen shouting "Fix, Fix, Fix" I picked him up and put him on my knee, he began to pick breakfast off my plate "so what is the plan for you lot today? It's nice outside why you don't go out for a nice walk" said Sue "or we could just bury you alive?" said Ben from behind us.

I just froze, Star, Sean, Karl just looked at me with a worried look on their faces as though he is going to tell her everything.

"Ben that's not very nice, I wish you boys would just get along", I made sure my Mum wasn't looking when I held out my arm behind me and pushed the Satan twins over with my wind power, they went crashing into the wall behind them.

"What's on earth is going on?" Sue said turning back around "we just fell over" Red said getting up of the floor and helping pull Ben up, "well you two need to be more careful you might hurt your selves".

After breakfast Star went home to talk to her brother, me, Sean and Karl went to my room to change and wait for Star.

Star never come back over that morning nor afternoon it was around 7 that evening when she appeared in my bedroom without Chadwick "I take it he said no?" "no, he said yes he just wanted me to tell you first that if it works then you leave the power of foresight with him and do not take it away from him".

"Of course, he can keep it, if it works then I would owe him and that's how I would repay him".

"That's what I told him" Star held up her phone and said "see Chadwick I told you he wouldn't take it away" she paused then hung up the phone, she held up one finger that represented one minute and she was gone "so how are you going to do it?" said Karl moving as far away as he could from where Star had appeared, I knew Karl didn't like Chadwick too much, I think it's his size that intimidates him. I shrugged my shoulders and replied "I don't really know but unless I try I would never know" Star and Chadwick both appeared, he had a hand on Stars shoulder "Felix" he said as soon as he saw me "Chadwick" I replied, "so where are we going to do this?" asked Chadwick "erm we can do it here if you want?" "whatever just do it quick," he said while scanning my room.

"Before we start how much has Star told you?" I asked getting up of my bed and sitting on the floor "I've told him everything, Felix, he needed to know it" "and I'm not to jazzed that you need to kill Annadora but she does need stopping so I'm going to try to help" Chadwick said sitting opposite me "ok I know it's hard but its what I have been told has been foreseen, I want to know if it's right and I need to know more details than that I have to just kill her".

"Ok what do I have to do?" he replied "exactly what you are doing, a few weeks ago while training with Star trying to use the energy power I had to feel her energy, hers feels

different to let's say Karl's and I just want to see what yours feels like.
That sounded a bit creepy I know but just bear with me",
we all sat in silence for around ten minutes, honestly, it felt longer. I closed my eyes trying to feel something.
I could feel Stars energy next to me and Sean and Karl's behind me I could feel Chadwick's energy, but it felt the same as all non-magical people, "I can't pick up on anything".
"I knew this was a waste of my time," Chadwick said getting up of the floor "wait Chadwick please just try again," Star said in a panicked tone.
"I think it's because there's too much energy in the room, Star take us to Drake Forest away from everyone and everything" and with that Star touched mine and Chadwick's shoulders and we were gone.
In Drake Forest Star took us to our regular training ground, it was dark and felt cold. The trees were swaying in the opposite direction to where the breeze was coming from.
"Star could you leave us both so it's just Chadwick's energy I can feel" "I don't know about that" Star said looking at me worried "it's ok Star I won't hurt your boyfriend" Chadwick chuckled.
I just looked at Star her face began to go red with embarrassment "I will be back in an hour" with that she disappeared.
I was a tiny bit afraid of being here alone with Chadwick, but I was the one that could protect myself, the thought of that made me feel a little more comfortable.
"Ok now just relax and open your mind to me" "and how the hell do I do that boy wonder?" "I don't know just relax and don't freak out if I have to touch you" I could see Chadwick getting mad "just relax, "I said as I closed my eyes.

I still could only feel normal energy flowing throw him so I reached forward and put my hand on top of his and he quickly pulled it away "I can't do this" Chadwick said getting up from the floor and pacing back and forth.
"I know it's hard" "how do you know it's hard, you're not me you have never lost something" "no I haven't lost anything, but I'm the one trying to get it back for you.
So just SIT DOWN AND LET ME TRY" I shouted the last part I was getting a little annoyed.
I was trying to help him. Instantly I regretted it as the reaction on Chadwick's face was of surprise and anger "please sit down" I said a little more softly, he did as he was told, he sat down with his legs crossed and his arms hanging down either side of him.
"Now please let me put my had on yours so the energy flows straight to me" Chadwick just nodded and held his right hand out and I took it like we were shaking hands.
The energy started to flow "just relax" I said closing my eyes "you do know every time you say that I can't relax" Chadwick laughed "shhh just relax" I said smiling "you nerd".
For what felt hours had passed I suddenly felt the smallest of sparks "there it is" I said.
"There's what?" "crap I've lost it, shhh I found it once I can find it again", "what was it like?".
"There was a spark, you know when you get a little shock from touching something, it was like that".
"Wow" Star made us both jump from behind me "Star how many times have I told you don't do that, Felix thinks he's found my foresight," Chadwick said excitedly.
"I know I heard" "go away and let Felix work his magic," Chadwick said waving her away, "ok, ok I will let you get back to work I just need a little boost from Felix, if that›s ok with you". She said while walking towards me.

"I'm fine with it," Chadwick said getting up and brushing all the dirt off the back of his legs "you have five minutes then he is mine," he said over his shoulder and he began to walk off, "so how's it going?" Star said holding my hand.

"Really, well now that he is opening up to me, what happened to him? how did he loose his power in the first place?" Star looked in the direction Chadwick had walked off, you could just make out where he was "our mother threw him of a six-story building when he was trying to save me from her" "six stories, how on earth did he survive?" I said rubbing my head.

"I saved him but not before his head hit the floor, I jumped down after him, but I was too late.

I broke his fall and broke my leg in the process when he landed on me. I took us back to our old house, me and my Dad tried to salvage what was left of his mind, we got most of it back, but the foresight was lost, we tried a few months later when he recovered but there was nothing of it left".

"That's terrible, I don't know what to say" I shook my head, how could a Mother throw their own child off a building.

We both watched Chadwick approach us, "That must be five minutes up by now" Chadwick said while sitting in the spot he has left not 5 minutes ago.

"Ok I get the picture, I will fill in Sean and Karl on your progress, when shall I come back?" Star asked, "give us another few hours," said Chadwick holding out his hand.

"Ok, see you two soon" then Star was gone, "ready," Chadwick said moving his hand closer towards me, I took it again just like before.

"Now just relax and do exactly what you were doing before when I found the spark", "I'll try" we closed are eyes I could feel the energy flow again.

It took longer than before to find the spark but when

I found it I said nothing as I didn't want Chadwick to stop whatever he was doing, I needed to hold on to that feeling.
"Anything?" Chadwick whispered "shhh" was my reply, so I slowly charged the spark, but it was taking forever it was as though it was faulty, it flicked on and then back off again. Star came back to take us home, it must have been around 5 am as the dark sky was lighting up with a tint of orange. The spark finally was fixed, it finally stayed on.
"How you boys getting on?" she asked looking between us both, "not very well I don't think" said Chadwick "hang on a second" I said with my eyes still closed and Chadwick's hand still in mine, they waited silently for me to finish.
All I was doing was connecting and disconnecting just to make sure the spark was still there I didn't want him to get his hopes up after another few connections I let go of Chadwick's hand and opened my eyes.
"Wow I ent half stiff," I said getting to my feet "well what happened? did you find it?" Chadwick asked in a disappointed tone, "yes I found it, it was faulty and misfiring that's why it took so long but I fixed it, now it stays on, so it should be easier to find when we try again".
"Thanks, Felix this means a lot to me," Star said giving me a massive hug, I berried my face in her hair and smelled it, 'mm coconut' "ok that's enough, Star you can take us back now".
Star let me go but still held my hand then grabbed Chadwick's, we were now back in my room. Star let go of my hand then they both were gone.
I told Sean and Karl about Chadwick's spark but all the way through telling them I couldn't stop yawning "this Chadwick business has drained me, I think I need to sleep" I said flopping on my bed.

I know Karl said something to me, but I was gone.

# CHAPTER 15

Ok so I slept and slept and slept I was asleep for nearly two days, when I finally woke up Sean and Karl had gone home but Star had stayed with me. "Good afternoon sleeping beauty" "how long was I out" "it's a little after two so only forty or so hours" "really?" I said getting up from my bed still in the same clothes as when I fell asleep.

Ouch, I was so stiff it hurt every time I moved, "wait there a second" Star said getting off her chair. She began to massage my back, it felt so good not because Star was doing it but my muscles were loosening up I felt so stiff. I jumped in the shower and pulled some clean clothes on, I felt like a human being again, me and Star went downstairs to grab some food as I was starving. Well, I had been asleep for two days, when we went downstairs I noticed no one was home, my Dad was most probably at work. The Satan twins were out as I couldn't hear their music and Mum must have taken Freddy to the park.

After eating four ham and cheese sandwiches, two sausage rolls and drank a whole six pack of coke in about ten minutes I started to feel myself, I could have eaten more but I could see Star starting to look sick so stopped.

"So, what did I miss when I was asleep?", "nothing really" "what about Chadwick how's he?" "his fine just apprehensive for you to wake up to work on him again. But I've told him that you are more important than his ability, so he has to wait until you are completely ready again, oh, I have to confess something" "ok what?" I asked confused "well I'm a hybrid as you like to call it so I tried to locate the spark you were talking about" "right did you find it?" "no there was nothing there, his head works just like a normal person does," Star said sheepishly like she shouldn't have said a thing.

"It's there but its deep I mean really deep" "there's nothing Felix I should have felt it" "I'm telling you it's there I will show you, take me to him or bring him to me" I was getting a little defensive about it and honestly a little annoyed that she didn't believe me, I know it's there.

In no time at all Star was back with Chadwick "now show me" she said, "what the hell is going on Star?" said Chadwick a bit disorientated.

"You know when I tried to find the spark yesterday, I couldn't find it well Felix is going to prove it", they both just looked at me "ok, not here, go to my room".

Once all three of us were in my room I sat on the floor with Chadwick in front of me and Star to the left of me, I took Chadwick's right hand again like before and closed my eyes "ok Chadwick like before just relax".

It didn't take me long to find the spark but it was misfiring again so that's probably why Star couldn't find it so I fixed it again, this time it shouldn't break, "can you feel it yet?" I asked still with my eyes closed after a long pause Star said, "no I can't".

I held out my left hand for her to hold, she didn't hesitate to take "how about now?" I tried to amplify the spark "wait, I can feel it, oh my god it's there, oh my god Felix" "I told you it's there but it was misfiring again and I've amplified it threw me so you could feel it but I told you its only tiny so I need to work on it some more".

"But you worked on it a few days ago and it knocked you out for two days" Star was right "what if I work an hour then rest?" "sounds good to me " Chadwick said before Star could answer.
"I will be fine, you can time us if you want" I joked
"don't forget that you need to train with fire before you get the earth element" she was right again "ok what about one day with Chadwick and then one day with you?" I said trying to please everyone.
"Ok but the first day is mine as I'm the oldest," Chadwick said, he sounded desperate for his power back "I will be back in an hour," Star said winking at me before vanishing, so for the next hour I worked on Chadwick's spark.
When Star turned up she had Sean and Karl in toe, so, we played games, talked like teenagers should, even Chadwick stayed and spent most the time with Karl chatting, after a few hours taking time out I went back to Chadwick.
The others didn't have to leave as I had a fix on exactly where it was, by 10 pm the spark had at least doubled in size so Star jumped Chadwick, Sean and Karl all home, I really need to call it something else than jumping, teleport that's the word I'm going to use from now on, jumping sounds as though they are jumping up and down.
I went to the bathroom to wash and change, looking in the mirror at my reflection was strange, I still look the same but there's all this power in me that I still can't get my head around. Walking out the bathroom fully dressed this time, I learn from my mistakes, Star was sitting there waiting for me "I thought we said one day with Chadwick and then one day with you" I said "we did but it's just habit coming here at night, I can go if you want me to?".
"No, no its fine, you can stay" I said the first no with a little volume, Star laughed and replied "I will be back in a

minute as your Mum is coming" then Star jumped, I mean teleported out, suddenly then there was a gentle knock at the door "Felix, are you awake?".
"Come in Mum" I said sitting on the edge of my bed "hello darling it feels like days since I last seen you" "a few too many late nights playing computer games, have you been out today" I asked trying to change the subject "I went to Jane's for a while then your Father met us there, the twins didn't want to come and you were asleep". "How is she?" "very well, Ken just brought a new car, some sort of Porsche, its bright yellow," said Sue with a little chuckle, I was surprised with the make, "wow sounds lush". "Ok night sweetheart it's getting late please don't be on the computer all night it's not good for you". "Ok Mum I won't put it on tonight, I will have a night off", "ok night Felix" "night Mum". She blew me a kiss just before leaving my room "blown kisses so sweet" said Star from behind me.
I tried not to jump but I failed and failed miserably, I jumped off my bed to the other side of my room grabbing my chest "that's it I'm defiantly getting you a bell", "oh don't be so mellow-dramatic" she replied.
"So, were you still here when my mum was in my room?" I asked while walking back over to my bed, "hybrid remember", "so what can you actually do?" I asked intrigued. "Well I take after my Dad more than my Mum, I'm more witch than fairy so I can do all sorts of things like jumping (teleport) to places, go invisible, chant spells and I have the same sort of wind power like yours but mine is just magic not an element power.
That's how I fought off Kayos". Just the mention of his name sends a shudder down my spine "why did he leave with her?" I asked but instantly regretted it as Star started crying, I quickly went over to her and put my arms around

her shoulders to comfort her "She. Told. Him. That. He. Can. Rule. All" Star said in-between sobs.
"It's ok, I don't know what it's like to be in a situation like that but I'm here and I will help in any way I can".
I didn't want to probe anymore "thank you, Felix," Star said wrapping her arms around my waist.
We stayed like that until Star stopped crying, her hair was now bright red, to help change it back I took some power away from her.
I changed the subject just as I did with my Mum, I laid on my bed while Star laid on her front propping her hear up with her hands, we just talked about random stuff. I tried to steer away from anything supernatural, by around 1 am we had both fallen asleep.
I was awoken by someone gently tugging at my arm, my eyes were still fuzzy but it looked like Karl "Karl is that you? what are you doing here?" "Yeah, it's me, your Mum let me in and good thing to as I think she would be a little bit shocked at this seen", suddenly, I twigged on to what Karl was saying, Star was still in bed with me fast asleep "oh crap, Star!" I whispered.
"Star you need to wake up sweetheart, Star," I said still whispering and shaking her just a little "what?" she said in a muffled and groggy voice.
"Star your still in my bed" "what!" Star said quickly getting up and out of the bed "what time is it?" "9:35 am" Karl replied looking at his watch.
"I better go, I will see you both a bit later". She lent down and gave me a peck on the cheek, "see you Karl" then she was gone.
"Well, Felix have you got something to tell me?" "like what?" I replied still disorientated, I felt as though I could sleep a few hours more, "oh, I don't know, what about the fact that

I just found you in bed with Star?" said Karl crossing his arms over his chest, "nothing happened Karl get your head out of the gutter".
"Well, then what happened?" "nothing we just talked then fell asleep, she has been coming to my room for a while now at night, its habit for her to come here", I could see that Karl was still skeptical but responded "ok well Sean said he will be here later he has got to do something with his Dad".
"I think we need a group meeting about getting the last element".
So, I texted Sean and Star the same message;

I didn't receive a reply from Sean, but he was with his Dad (sheriff Grady) where there is a high chance that he is not allowed to take his phone with him, but I knew he was in.
I had to go to hell to talk to the Satan twins it's not a pleasant experience in their room, but I had to go in to speak to them.
I knocked on their door as loud as I could, so they could hear over their music, it opened just enough for Ben to poke his head out "What?" he asked "there's going to be a meeting in my room at 4" "and?" he replied as though I was putting him out by inviting him "be here" I said getting annoyed.

"We don't have to be there" "well if you're not there then you're out" "you just can't throw us out like that, we know too much," said Red opening the door wider "and who are you going to tell Red? Mum? Dad?" well that shut them up.

"Just be there at four," I said walking off "bloody morons," I said under my breath "who's a moron?" said my Dad, walking up the stairs.

"No one how come you haven't opened the store?"

"it's Wednesday" "oh yeah I forgot," I said hitting me palm to my forehead as I knew he didn't open the shop till 12 pm on a Wednesday, he hasn't done so since like forever! "Dad, can I talk to you a minute about something?" "of course, you can son what's up?".

I really didn't know what to say to him, but I was just curious what he knows about Great Granddad Felix.

"Can we talk in my room?" I asked as I began to walk in the direction of my room "sure", so he followed in behind me, Karl was sitting on the end of my bed waiting for my return. He was a little shocked when Phil was behind me "Mr. Moon" said Karl politely "hello Karl I didn't see you come in" "Mrs. Moon let me in" he said sitting uncomfortably, "ok Dad I want to ask you something" "you sure you want to do this with an audience?" he asked looking directly at Karl.

"He knows what's going on, I know it's a bit out of the blue but what was Great Granddad Felix like?".

"Well, he was a great man, always telling these story's just like the ones that I told you when you lot was younger".

"Did he ever mention avatars in any of the story's?" "where's this going Felix?" I could see Karl looking at me in the corner of my eye "what about Alicade or Aries or what about Baltazar?" I probed, I could see Karl's mouth now gapped open.

“Stop Felix, where are you getting all this from?” “Dad just give it up, I know you know a lot more than the story’s you told us as kids, Annadora is not just a fairy Princess gone bad, she is an avatar as well.

Now tell us the unedited version” I couldn’t believe I just asked him all of it, but it needed to be asked. “If I tell you, will you tell me how you know these things?” crap that meant I had to tell him that I was an avatar, ‘ok I will tell him that I’m an avatar but I won’t tell him that I’m a mod avatar and that I have to die by the element to possess it that would shock and worry him’ “deal”.

The story was quite gruesome most of the story we already knew but the parts that were missed out was 99% of the killings and how she did it, I won’t tell you as I don’t want to give you nightmares, but I now know and wish I hadn’t. Me and Karl were sitting on the bed and Phil was sitting on the computer chair that was pulled up to the bed “so now that you know everything are you going to tell me how you know all this?” Phil asked leaning back in the chair “well... I was told... erm... I’m an avatar of sorts” Phil’s eyes nearly popped out of his head.

“Did I hear you right? did you just say that you are an avatar?” I just nodded “who on earth would tell you that?”.

“Ok well here’s the thing when I was given a power I appeared in a white room and I spoke to someone called Aries, he trained me to use the element that I had just possessed, then....” I didn’t know If I should tell him that Great-Granddad Felix was an avatar too “go on” Phil said sitting forward in the chair, he was intrigued I could tell by his facial expressions “ok well Great Granddad Felix was an avatar as well, wasn’t he?” my Dad just froze, that was my sign that he never knew the truth.

"Erm I don't know what to say" "Dad I know this is a lot to take in but, in the story, something got taken from her, it was this?", I walked over to my bed and pulled a draw from underneath, I reached in and pulled out the blood red crystal.

"This is Annadora's Crybecker, this is where most of her power is, Great Granddad Felix gave it to me when I was 6" I handed it to my Dad. He just sat there looking at it for ages then handed it back and asked, "so do you have one of those?" I handed it to Karl for him to look at it as well, I don't think he got to see it properly before.

"No, I don't as I have all the energy already in me" "apart from earth" Karl butted in still twisting the Crybecker in his fingers 'oh please Karl shut your gob' "that's right Karl I don't have earth yet it hasn't manifested yet" I said taking the Crybecker from him and sent him a killer stare that meant 'shut the hell up'. Karl opened his mouth but then thought better of it, "and when will the earth manifest itself?" asked Phil still trying to get his head around that his son and his Grandfather are avatars.

"How did you know you were an avatar?" "I don't really know, it just kind of happened" "so can you use your powers? Can you show me?" "yes, I can show you, what do you want to see?" "you said you don't have the earth element, show me how you use water?", I nodded and I held my hand towards the water on my bedside table and made it float out of the glass. I directed it to hover over my Dad's head, then I let it sprinkle down over him, so it looked like it was raining, "wow, that's amazing, show me something else", I showed him as wind orb, letting it float around the room, I clicked my fingers and made fire, "oh my god, think I'm at my limit with what I can take in right now, we will have to talk again later" he said while standing up.

“Dad all I say is please don’t tell Mum she will only worry and go crazy” “there’s not a chance that I will tell her, even if I did she would probably think I’m telling my own fairy tales” “Thanks Dad” I replayed.
Once the door was closed Karl turned to me and said “oh my god Felix I thought his head was going to explode, but you could have given me a heads up on what you were doing” “it was a spur of the moment thing, I knew he wasn’t telling us all the story, I had a feeling that he knew more than he was letting on”.
After getting washed and dressed and went downstairs with Karl for some food and before we knew it, it was 4 pm and the Satan twins were just walking into my room “what do you want?” asked Red “we have to wait for Sean and Star to come”.
“We are here, I found this stray outside,” Star said from behind me with Sean and Chadwick. That was a shock as I didn’t think he wanted anything to do with this, what do I call it? a quest? or task? “hey Chadwick, Red close the door” he did as he was told and shut the door.
“So, my Dad now knows half of what’s going on here, he knows that I’m an avatar, but he does not know that I have to die by it to get the power. So, we need to keep that from him, that’s all he knows so nothing about dying and he knows a little about Annadora but he doesn›t need to know all of it.
He doesn’t know about you two ether, it’s not my secret to tell” “thanks Felix so what’s happening with the last possession?” Star asked, “well that’s where Red and Ben come in” “we have been ready since the fire so we are ready when you are”.
“This weekend? Sunday? ok for everyone?” they all nodded together “it’s a date”.

't after it was agreed "so talk me through
with these possessions you have?" asked
I have to die by the element like I was drowned" "Kayos, Kayos found Felix and tried to kill him, I stopped him" Star said sitting next to me on the bed "and once my heart stops I go to a room" "what kind of room?" Chadwick butted in "well it's all white with nothing in it, that's where Aries trains me with that power but the last time our meeting didn't go down so well, he's the one that told me that Its been foreseen that I kill...." "my Mother" Chadwick finished my sentence.

"You're what?" Sean asked in a raised voice "mine and Stars Mother is Annadora" I just sat there still not saying a thing with my hand covering my mouth, my eyes as wide as they will go, afraid to blink, "your Mother is Annadora?" Sean asked bewildered, Chadwick nodded "Felix did you know this?" Karl whispered still sat to the other side of me "yes I did, Aries told me". "And you think that we didn't need to know that little nugget of information?" Sean said getting angry.

"Felix why didn't you tell us," Karl said he looked hurt and betrayed "I told him not to say anything as I didn't want you to think bad of me" "Star is right, I didn't say because she asked me not to, so now what? you want out? Sean? Karl?" Sean didn't say anything he just stood there at the window looking at Star like he was trying to figure out what to say "I'm still in but you should have told us" Karl said getting up from the bed and walking over to Sean "come on Sean lets go get some fresh air" Sean stormed out the room and went downstairs, I could hear the front door close as he left the house. "I will talk him around" Karl then left following Sean.

"Sorry, that was my fault I should keep things to myself"

"it's ok Chadwick it was bound to come out sooner or

later" "but still I think I should leave to, Star take me hom please". "Why don't you use the door?" she said in a short snap "let's think about it, err maybe because I never came through the bloody door in the first place, I think Felix's parents will be a bit suspicious" "that's true, I will be back in a second" Star reached out and touched Chadwick's arm then were both gone.

I got up from the bed and opened the window and began to look out, it was beginning to get dark. Suddenly, there was a little knock at the door, "fix" so I knew straight away it was Freddy so I let him in "come in mini-me" it was nearly bedtime so Freddy run in and jumped on my bed and got comfy under the blanket but before I could start to walk over to him to tuck him in Star appeared in front of me and said "ready for some training?".

"Fix" Star froze in place, what on earth do I tell him? I know his only 3 but hell, she just materialized in front of him, "it's ok Freddy, Star is magic same as me, look" I said sidestepping Star that is still frozen to the spot, so I showed him a wind orb, as that's the easiest to show him without mega freaking him out, Freddy sat up and reached for the ball.

This time I could let him as I was in 100% control of it, I even put it in his hands "it's ok Star his fine now" I said trying to ease her fear. She slowly turned around "I'm so sorry I completely forgot it's that time of night," Star said crouching at the side of the bed.

"It's fine, look at him, he's having fun" Freddy was fascinated with the wind orb but it was bedtime, so I told Freddy to clap his hands and with a poof the wind was gone, he gave me a quick hug and snuggled up in my bed.

Me and Star sat on the floor under the window "you would do anything for that little boy wouldn't you?" "I don't know

why but it's like I have to protect him with everything I have, it's always been like it from the day he was born. It's a little bit like it with you" I could see her in the corner of my eye looking at me, but I just stayed focused at Freddy.
"Why do you have it with me?" Star asked in a low whisper,
"I don't know, I really don't" Star leaned her head on my shoulder "it's ok, we will figure it out" she replied.
"I know like everything else" I lent my head on top of hers, we stayed like it for ages, I could see Star's hair started to change red, I didn't want to move but I knew we should.
"Your Mums coming again," she said, "don't go, just do that invisible thing" Star just smiled and nodded then she was gone, "Felix! is Freddy in there?" I quickly got up off the floor and opened the door "yeah he is asleep" "thanks Felix what would I do without you" Sue said picking Freddy up off my bed and cradling him.
"Felix I just wanted to tell you that your Father and I are taking Freddy to the lake next weekend, would you like to come?" "maybe," I said as there's a lot going on my plate right now and a holiday to Lake Halo wasn't on the cards. Sue left, and Star reappeared "you know Felix a holiday away from all this might be good for you" but I didn't answer her as I was deep in thought 'Lake Halo, Lake Halo why Lake Halo? why do I want to go there?' "Baltazar," I said aloud and bolted for the door "what?" Star said but I was gone.
I found Sue in the kitchen (shocker) "hey Mum I've been thinking that a trip to the lake sounds nice" "wow that's great" "cool, can't wait" I said grabbing some food from the fridge that could feed 6 people, but I wasn't sure what Star likes to eat so a bit of everything will do "hungry? I can make you some dinner" she questioned.
"No thanks Mum this will do". I was taking the stuff back to my room when there was a knock at the door, I just stood

on the stairs while Sue opened the door to wait to see who it was, it was Sean and Karl "come in lads, Felix is just going upstairs with some food that could feed a small army" "thanks Mrs. Moon" they both said together.
They both followed me into my room, picking up all the food I dropped on the way and closing the door behind them. Star was perched on the window sill with her arms crossed against her chest with an angry face on 'god she looks so cute angry' I thought to myself "look, I brought you some food" I tried to sound friendly and happy. "Why did you run out of the room saying 'Baltazar' and not explain why?" "Oh, have we come at a bad time?" Karl said with a little laugh, I think it was nervous laugh "ok I will explain" I said dropping the food on the bed and holding my hands out in surrender, "my parents are going to Lake Halo and that's where I think they're holding Baltazar" "are you going to look for him?" Karl said stepping forward.
I just nodded "that's crazy, you can't," Star said getting angrier "but if I find him he might give me some answers about being a mod avatar?" "I think Felix is right," Sean said "his not getting the right answers from the other side as I don't think they know what a mod avatar can actually do, what have they got to go on? Baltazar? An evil avatar but Felix ent like that, we won›t let him" "thanks Sean" "I still think it›s too risky" Star said, "what do you think Karl?" we all were looking at him "erm well I think it's your decision".
"We are in this all together," I said putting my hand on his shoulder "I'm with... Star, we just don't know what will happen, sorry" "it's ok mate I want your true opinion not for you to just go along with everything, what about Chadwick? what if I get his foresight working in time? he could foresee it".

"That might work but how long do you think it will take to give Chadwick's power of foresight?" "I will probably have to work every day" "well that's not going to work, is it? you worked on him for a few hours and slept for two days" Star said, "crap that's right" "could that be because you're not a full mod avatar?" Karl asked.

We all were silent for a minute all lost in thought, Star broke the silence first "he might be right" so we discussed what we were going to do, I would work on Chadwick as much as I could without getting too drained, my training will have to have a back foot to this plan but tonight we train and Star wanted to work on the energy power as that's the one I'm going to be using a lot of.

Sean and Karl came to Drake Forest with us, Karl freaked out a little, but he knew it was for a good corse. As like before Star would cover my eyes and I had to sense her but now with Sean and Karl here it was a little harder but I did it, there's just the tiniest of difference between them all, Star's energy felt like a deep hum but with a spark running through it, Sean's had a deep hum with a deeper pulse running through it and Karl's had the same hum but had a slightly higher pulse running through it.

After training finished Star took me home then took them both to their houses.

They had their task to do, they had to look for something/ somewhere that might resemble a place that could hold Baltazar at Lake Halo.

So that's all I did until Sunday was work on Chadwick and his spark, it was hard to work on it, as it seemed to drain me quicker and quicker, by Saturday his spark was big enough that Star could feel it without my help.

Waking up Sunday morning I felt horrible, for some reason the earth element possession scared me. This was different than the others I am going to be buried alive, with the fire possession I could have bailed from the box and with the wind and water possession I didn't even know about them one's when it happened. But this one I was alone, no one could help me.

The day was going really fast, the only day I wanted to go slow it wouldn't, by 3 pm I had bitten all my nails down till they hurt, the Satan twins were out before I got up.

That was good I suppose as I knew full well they would remind me about it every five minutes, the only reprieve I had from my strange new life was Freddy, we played all morning together. We coloured, played with his cars, played out side with a ball and swam in our pool.

I didn't want it to end but I knew it had to, when Star tuned up with Chadwick at the front door, I held up one finger telling them 'just one minuet'. I went into the living room where I left Freddy asleep on the sofa and kissed him gently on the forehead as not to wake him.

In the kitchen my Mum was cooking, dancing away from cupboard to cupboard humming "oh Felix, you frightened me" Sue said holding her hand up to her heart "sorry Mum I just wanted to tell you that I'm going out and I'm not sure what time I will be back.

I might even stay over at Sean's" "ok sweetie just give me a call if you do, ok" "will do Mum" I gave her a kiss on the cheek and walked out my front door to meet with Star and Chadwick.

# CHAPTER 16

When we got to the 'site' Sean, Red and Ben were there holding shovels I could see a hole that they had dug, it looked huge and deep, well at least I knew what Red and Ben have been up to all day.
Anyone would think they can't wait to bury me alive!
There was a box that I had to get into, next to the hole "I think that's a bit small" I said pointing at the box "we made it small, so you die quicker" said Red a little too cheerful.
I lost it, my breathing began to change, and I felt as though I was gasping for breath "I can't do this, I can't" then I bolted towards the woods "Felix, FELIX" everyone was shouting and chasing after me, but I outrun them and hid in a dead tree.
I stayed there for what felt like hours not moving, I could feel my phone vibrating in my pocket, but I didn't want to talk to anyone, none of them knew what I'm going through. They don't have to die "Felix, where are you?" it was Star I could hear calling, my heart broke as I could hear the pain in her voice, I stood up and began to get out of the tree "Star" I said in a low voice, she found me, she walked over and gave me the biggest hug, tears streaming down her face.
"Felix" I put my arms around her and let her cry.
A few minutes later I whispered, "Star your hair is going red"
"I don't care" Star said pulling me tighter, her hair was bright red now, so I pulled away a little "why did you run?" "I'm

scared Star, like really scared to the point I want to go home and hide from everything and everyone I don't know if I can do this one".

"Felix we are here for you, you know this, why didn't you just talk to one of us?" Star said letting go and stepping back, she whipped her eyes with the cuff of her sleeve.

"How can I talk to you or anyone about dying, no one else has done it, let alone three times already" "I don't know about dying but we can talk it out, about anything" I sat down on a fallen tree "Star just give me a minute to think, there's so much stuff going on in my head, everything is jumbled up and I can't think straight".

"Ok Felix but before I go please can you take some of this energy, I can feel it running through me too fast" Star said standing in front of me, I just nodded and took her hand and pulled some the energy out of her until the ends of her hair was blonde, I then let go and put my face in my hands.

Star kissed the top of my head and said "I will see you soon" then she was gone.

I was there for another hour before I got up and started heading back the way I ran.

Back at the 'site', Sean was on the phone to Karl I suspect, Red and Ben were standing in the hole talking about something but when they saw me they quickly jumped out really quick.

I didn't even look for Star and Chadwick "back, are you? not going to freak out again?" Red laughed as if it was funny that I had to die off one of the most horrible deaths. I just looked at him and said "do it now before I change my mind" I didn't even look at Star as I knew that I wouldn't go through with it once I saw her face.

I threw my phone and keys on the floor and got in the box, I shut my eyes once the lid was on I could sense it got much

darker, I put my hands over my face and started crying like a big girl with sobs and all.
I just hoped that they couldn't hear me, I could feel them lift me up then lower me in the hole, I hit the floor with a little bump and heard someone say 'sorry' I think it was Sean. "Does anyone want to say any words?" I heard muffled "JUST GET ON WITH IT" I shouted getting annoyed when I heard the first lot of dirt hit the box I was in full freak out mode. I was short of breath, I was hyperventilating, I still had my hands over my face and that's all I remember as I must have blacked out when I come too, everything was white.
"Oh, look the white room, oh goodies," I said to myself no one turned up for hours, so I trained alone with earth power 'how hard can it be' I thought, well I was wrong I couldn't do a thing. I tried so hard for what felt like ages then suddenly there was a bright light in the corner of the room.
It was my Great Granddad Felix, we hugged and spoke about the earth power, he said that I had to have earth on me to be able to bend it, as we were in a white room with no earth in I couldn't move any, so we practiced the others altogether.
"Granddad, I have a confession to make, I told my Dad about us" "whys that my boy?" he asked in a low tone "I was asking him about the story's you told him and he begged me to tell him so I did, I'm sorry" "it's ok I was going to tell him but I died before I could" said Granddad Felix.
I felt a little relieved that I didn't spill any state secrets, "have you spoken to Aries?" "I have, and he was very shaken, what you did wasn't very nice" "well if he would have let me leave when the room was spinning I wouldn't have gone to drastic measures," I said getting mad.
"Felix there's no need to get angry" "why? why can't I get angry? you nor Aries told me everything about being a mod

avatar you never mentioned about having five powers".
"Ok Felix I know we never told you everything, we just wanted to protect you," said Granddad Felix "if you wanted me to kill Annadora then I would of thought you would have told me everything to make it easier for me".
"Yes, I understand that, but the energy power is a mystery to us, Baltazar was the only one with that possession, so we knew nothing about it", "then why don't you ask me?" I replied.
"I don't understand?" "ask me what it's like? what it's like to have the energy power?" "ok, Felix what is it like having the energy power?" "it's fantastic, I've helped so many people, like Freddy, he was sick and I helped him and when Star needs a boost of power" "Felix I told you to stay away from that girl and her family" Granddad Felix interrupted. I thought it was best not telling him that I'm helping Chadwick get his foresight back "but she's the one getting me through all this madness.
Once I'm out of here I'm all alone with no one to help me, but Star is, she's helping me train with all these powers and there's no one that can stop me. Will, you try stopping me, Granddad Felix?".
"Felix this is not healthy, your heart is getting dark, I can feel it" that last bit took me back 'my heart is getting dark' "what do you mean by that?" "what you did to Aries was a sign, you took his powers away Felix". "Well he shouldn't have tried to trap me here, my time was up here, and I needed to leave, and he wouldn't let me so I showed him who's boss" Granddad Felix grabbed my arm tight and said in my ear through gritted teeth "listen to yourself Felix, you are even starting to sound dark". I couldn't say anything as it was true, I couldn't let it happen to me, I had too much depended on me.

"What do I need to do to stop me going over to the dark side?" "stop seeing that Redfield girl" "I can't do that" "you have to Felix, she is the one taking you down that path" Granddad Felix gripped my arm tighter "NO" I shouted and pulling my arm away with such force that he had to take a step back to steady himself.
"The only ones I see taking me down that path is you lot not telling me everything I need to know"
"it's in her blood, it's inevitable that she will follow in her Mother's footsteps". "I can't leave her, I'm bound to her somehow, ever since I met her I've been pulled to her, it's not as bad as the pull I have to Freddy. It's like I have to protect them with everything I have".
That shut Granddad Felix up for a bit. "bound you say?" repeated Granddad Felix deep in thought, "do you know what that means?" I asked as I was intrigued to know if he knew why, "Felix this is not good", "please share with the class, what does it mean?" I was getting a little agitated now. "It means she's the one" "she's the one what?" "she's the one for you, she is your forever" then I twigged what he was going on about "oh right!" I felt embarrassed I could feel my face going red. I knew I liked her but being told that she's 'the one' and 'my forever' was fine with me, I don't know how Star is going to take it.
"I understand now with Star but why do I have it with Freddy and its worse with him, it's not because his 'the one' as he is three and my kid brother," I said still a little confused "I don't know that one Felix, I really don't".
I could start to hear my name being called faintly so I knew it was nearly time for me to go "will I ever come back here?" "yes, now that you are a full avatar you can come and go as you please" "cool, just one more question, do you know what this is?" I said pulling my top up and showing him the

mark that's showing up on my back "Felix that's the mod avatar mark" the room was spinning so fast I dropped to my knees and there was a loud piercing noise so loud that I had to cover my ears to try and stop it, It was that loud it felt like my head was going to explode.
The noise subsided, and I was still in the white room with Granddad Felix, he was lying next to me with his hand over his ears "what the hell was that?" I shouted. There was blood trickling down from Granddad Felix's ears, looking in my hands there was blood on them too.
"Felix are you ok?" "yes, what was that?" "I don't know" he replied with a worried look on his face "why am I still here? I was leaving" "the portal looks to be broken" "what the hell does that mean? am I stuck here?" "Sorry, but yes I think so". Great, what does that mean, was I stuck here, forever? "Granddad Felix, didn't you say that avatars can come in and out of this world?" "yes, they can but through the portal, with no portal, no one can come here or leave. Come on Felix let's see what's going on" then in a flash we were covered in a bright white light and we were gone.
The sight in front of me was breathtaking, I will try and describe it but I know whatever I say won't give it the justices it needs, there were crystals everywhere I think most of the houses were made out of the stuff in all different colours and in the middle, was a massive shard of crystal all in white they all glistened in the sunlight surrounded by a good 10 ft, of what looked like a wall of water rolling up then back down behind it. "Welcome to Alicade Felix", I was speechless I wanted to see this place but not now. If I was here that meant I was dead in the real world "am I dead?" I asked worried, I could feel my breathing change slightly, so I tried to breathe in and out steadily to calm myself down.
"Yes and no, in the other world you are but here you are

not", "can I ever go back?".
"I'm sorry Felix but that's not possible" "but what if the portal gets fixed?" "there's no way of knowing Felix as your body is dead on the other side and it might be months or even years before it can be fixed, but the question is who broke the portal in the first place?" Granddad Felix began walking down the hill.
I willed my feet to move but they were glued to the spot where I stood.
"Come on Felix, it's not safe out here" still I couldn't move, Granddad Felix walked back up the hill and pulled me with him. I don't even remember how we got through the wall of water and into the crystal shard in the middle of the city, but we were here.
"Felix this place is called Falkor," he said, but all I was thinking was that I was dead, Sean, Star, Ben, Red, Chadwick and Karl even though he wasn't there they will all be freaking out as I was dead, what about my parents? what will they do when they find out? Freddy "no, no, NO, I'm not dead I need to go back" I was losing it "calm down Felix, we will get to the bottom of this King Brogue will know", "I can't stay here, what about what's been foreseen? if I'm here how can I kill Annadora?".
"FELIX, just calm down, we will talk to King Brogue" I was still freaking out but only on the inside. We walked through these big dark green doors into a huge room with tall white columns that looked sharp to the touch and right at the other end of the room was a dark green (just like the doors) throne that could sit three people comfortably but there was only one man sitting on it.
He was wearing the same kind of toga dress thing but his was jet black that matched his hair "King Brogue, please a word?".

“Of course, Felix my friend” he nodded in my direction as though he was greeting me.
“We have a problem, the portal is broken” the room fell silent “how do you know this?” said a scrawny man standing next to the King, I don’t get a good feeling from him he looks shifty, you know when you look in to someone’s eyes and you feel like they are robbing you while you are stood in front of them, yeah that feeling.
“Well this is my Great Grandson Felix and he is stuck here, he couldn’t go back” “and I don’t want to stay here any longer than needed, shall we try and fix this?” “hold your tongue boy,” said Mr creepy, “it’s ok Jani, he’s only worked up and wants to go home,” said the King.
There was screaming coming from somewhere but I couldn’t place it “Jani, Kava go find out what’s going on, Felix and Jr come with me” he stood up from his throne and began to walk, we followed him behind the throne to a door in the back that led to a tunnel, he began to run, both Granddad Felix and I both followed suit at the end was another door “where are we going?” I asked looking back to where we had come from “we are going to the library” the King said pushing the doors open.
There were books from floor to ceiling, there must be hundreds of thousands of them “wow” “I love to read, we will be safe in this room” I couldn’t work out just how these books were to save us but I’d be happy to read a few of them. We waited and waited, the King and my Granddad Felix talked while I went looking at the books while scanning the titles I come across a book about foresight.
I took the book to a chair in the corner and started to read, it was so interesting it said that something that has been foreseen is not a fixed point in time and it is possible to change the outcome but its advised that what has been

foreseen plays it course and does not change.
I got halfway through the book when there was a knock at the door "King Brogue" Granddad Felix opened the door and it was Jani "the portal is broken, and we are under attack by Annadora's men and her son". "Kayos" I asked panicking and dropped the book I was holding onto the floor, as the last time we met didn't end very well.
"We need to get you out of here and to the Glacier where it's safe", "go, Granddad, protect the King I will say and fight, I'm a mod avatar, I'm better needed here".
"No Felix I'm not leaving you" "what's the worst that can happen? I'm dead already".
So that's what happened I stayed after we hugged, and they left. I fort alongside Kava, he showed me so much in the way of fighting tactics and concentration.
I was stuck in Alicade for 6 years 9 months and 21 days fighting, not that I was counting or anything, I was posted at the portal while they fixed it, but it was long going.
When the day finally comes when the portal was fixed I was unsure if I wanted to go back, but when I thought of Freddy my heart sank and I needed to go, it wasn't a choice.
"Are you sure you won't reconsider my offer and stay?" asked King Brogue, "it is a fantastic offer to be head of the guard, but I think I'm needed more out there". "Ok you will be greatly missed, and the offer will always be open for you, please come and visit" "thanks".
Granddad Felix took me back to the white room and we just stood there looking at each other, it was planned but as though we were prolonging the inevitable.
"Can I ask you something?" "anything" he replied, I stood there facing him all serious "when I go back to my body, will I be a zombie? all green and my skin all falling off and my bones showing threw?" "wow Felix you have a very

vivid imagination, I've been told your body will be perfectly preserved".
"I will miss you so much Granddad," I said giving him a hug, I could feel my self-welling up "I will miss you too my boy, don't forget you can visit now whenever you want".
"I will keep that in mind, wow I forgot that the room spins so fast," I said falling to my knees "bye Granddad" but I was gone before he could reply.

To Be Continued......

Hello, I'm Carla Pearson, I've always loved writing little stories for myself for a long time.

Since my nieces and nephews started growing up, I wanted to write a story for them to read so here is my chance.

I would like to thank my family and friends for the love, support and encouragement that they all have gave me while writing my story's, I've literally been a hermit for months, all work and no play.

I would like to thank my nephew Elliott for reading the story first and becoming my first official fan.
I would also like to thank my sister Laura for all the hard work she has put into the book too and for keep pushing me to do my best.

I've suffered from dyslexia most of my life, but it hasn't stopped me from writing this book and the others that are yet to come.

I will never overcome my dyslexia, but writing has really helped me with my reading and spelling skills. I would also be great if one of my book inspires others to achieve their dreams.

I wouldn't say the book is perfect, it's my first one so I'm still learning, thanks for taking the time to read it.

It would be amazing if you would take the time to follow me, also please leave feedback it would be great to read what you think of my book.

Facebook: https://www.facebook.com/carlaannpearson/
Twitter: https://twitter.com/Carla_A_Pearson
Instagram: https://www.instagram.com/carla_a_pearson/
Goodreads: https://www.goodreads.com/user/show/88276668-carla-pearson

Much Love x

www.ingramcontent.com/pod-product-compliance
Ingram Content Group UK Ltd.
Pitfield, Milton Keynes, MK11 3LW, UK
UKHW021050270726
13967UKWH00012B/191

9 781912 641994